THE SUM OF ITS PARTS

RICHARD ZWICKER

*Thanks to the many writers in Critters.org
who have critiqued my work over the years.*

THE SUM
OF
ITS PARTS

CONTENTS

1 Monsters All 1

2 The Monster Is the Father to the Child 13

3 Before the Beginning 23

4 Voodoo as I Say 35

5 None So Blind as Those Unseen 49

6 What Lies Beneath the Bandages 71

7 Wherefore Art Thou, Werewolf 93

8 The Sum of Its Parts.............................. 105

1

Monsters All

FOR MONTHS I LED Victor Frankenstein on a mad chase, from Switzerland to Italy to Russia to the Arctic Ocean. Then a storm separated us and, in the distance, I watched a passing ship rescue my creator and leave me for dead. I didn't mind the "left for dead" part, but I refused to allow outsiders to settle our conflict.

As I sailed to the ship's stern, the night was black as the bottom of the sea, and with the buffeting wind, only marginally drier. I bound an oar with rope and tossed it multiple times over the ship's rail. When it held, I secured the other end to my single-sailed craft and scaled the hull, unseen. Creeping into the cabin area, I felt my way through the darkness, using the salt-encrusted wall as a guide. The walls creaked like a soul on a rack, complemented by an array of snores, some harsh like a saw, others like a gentle puff off a cigar. I felt lost, until a familiar voice said, "Damned monster, I will chase thee to the gates of hell." Had I not been drenched, my ears would have been burning.

I turned into the room where my nemesis lay twisting on a hammock. "Victor, the time has come," I said, but as I touched his boiling forehead, I knew the time had passed. The handsome, virile scientist had turned into a scarecrow. After all our travails, we now met in this most unnatural place as equal monsters. In his sunken eyes I saw recognition of me and the importance of the moment. His scarred lips fluttered to form a final message. Out of respect and curiosity, I waited.

"I hate you," he whispered, and died. *Same to you,* I wanted to say, but my anger had lost its object, and I instead emitted a soul-wrenching groan. Moments later, a hulking man carrying a lantern appeared in the doorway.

"You!" he said.

I'd been called much worse, but he didn't stop there.

"Damned monstrosity! Demon! Misbegotten spawn of hell! Victor has told me everything. As my name is Captain Robert Walton, you will pay!" He spat out his words through his bearded face, shaking in anger.

"Indeed, I will. Victor's pain is over."

"What? You killed him?"

"I suppose. He died in childbirth."

"What the devil are you talking about?"

There was no point in continuing. My intention was to jump back onto my craft and drift from all that was natural, but Walton had other ideas. He yelled for his men. The sleepers awoke, and sets of feet banged onto the floor, echoing like cannon shot. I struck the captain in the face, and he crumbled into a heap, then I tore back onto the deck. Aided by the darkness and the sleep-befuddled pursuers, I grabbed my oar and sprang over the side. Sputtering, I pulled myself onto my boat and rowed like a galley slave. Apparently, my being off the ship satisfied Walton, and I was not pursued further.

For days I sailed north. Without landmarks, I saw no progress. I figured my voyage would end with my boat lodged in ice or me drowned. Though I thought Victor's best revenge would be for me to live and suffer for my sins, the Arctic Ocean wasn't the greatest place for atonement. Just remaining afloat required near-constant attention, allowing but snatches of sleep. The harsh cold and drenching waves tormented my body. I had neither time nor energy to dwell on past transgressions.

One day clouds and mist, thick as cataracts, filled the air. The ocean roared in my ears. Waves separated me from the air I struggled to breathe. I grasped for purchase of anything that might keep me alive. You might ask why I didn't surrender, but I believed my one chance at purification lay in defiance, until I could defy no more. I bound myself with rope to my boat, but the knots kept loosening, and I was tossed into the bracing sea. Each time my resolve and everything else stiffened as I lugged myself back atop my battered craft.

Time has no meaning in a tempest, and as my muscles failed, I felt the shelter of detachment. I could no longer hear the wind or feel the slaps of the swells. I willed the swirling mist into mental pictures I could grasp, such as living in the abandoned house where I discovered my love of books, or when the old blind man befriended me. These images never lasted long, however, and eventually all coalesced into an approaching ship. At first, I thought Captain Walton had taken pity on me, but this ship looked older, with torn sails and curved masts.

Who knows why, but with a choice, I now wanted to live. I furiously paddled toward the ship, making progress, as if the sea had opened a path. The ship ranged eighty yards long, with three masts, and it glowed as if lit by a hundred candlesticks. From the deck a silent man, with a long salt and pepper beard protruding from under his cap, lowered a rope. I hadn't the strength to climb, so I tied the rope around my waist while he and another man hoisted me on board. I fell flat on the deck like a fish gasping for breath. I pulled myself upright, and then, despite my former ambivalence about living, showered my benefactors with thanks. In a fierce storm, they'd gone out of their way to help a stranger, and I would find a way to repay them. When neither man said a word, I gazed closer at them.

Their clothes hung tattered on their bodies, stiffened with salt. The matted hair on their heads and lined faces stuck out like tentacles. The mist gave their bodies a wispy, insubstantial look. Like the ship, a dull glow emitted from their bodies, as if the mist reflected a source of light, or perhaps my ordeal had scrambled my senses.

What manner of people rescues a drowning man only to ignore him? I reached for the sinewy arm of a passing crewman but grabbed only air. I sat back dumbfounded, as if tricked by a cape-waving matador.

As the silent sailors walked away, I stumbled to my feet and followed one at a discreet distance. I passed crewmen doing typical tasks. Several swabbed the deck. Another sat cross-legged, repairing a net. Yet another stood stoically at the wheel. None paid me any attention. I knew the loneliness of the high seas and how when ships intersected, both crews took the opportunity to converse. Even if the men on this ship were taciturn by nature, my seven-foot-tall body and flat head should have elicited a raised eyebrow. But my presence made no more impact on them than a coiled rope. I was not of their world.

My aloof guide led me below deck, where an ever-present soft glow painted the darkness. He stopped in front of a door, opening it to reveal a small room. I stuck my head inside and saw a full-bearded man seated at an otherwise deserted table. In front of him lay a yellowed piece of paper with rows of numbers etched upon it. I was not surprised when he failed to acknowledge me. I waited a moment then sat opposite him in one of two empty chairs.

"My name is ..." I didn't have a name, so I took the only one that made any sense. "Frankenstein."

For the first time, he gazed at me. In his eyes I detected no twinkle or discernment. He reached into his pants pocket, pulled out a handful of folded letters, and placed them in front of me. I remembered the *Flying Dutchman* legend, a ghostly crew doomed to sail the world. Whenever it encountered a ship, it handed to the living crew letters to deliver, usually to people long dead. To receive such a letter was generally a portent of doom.

"I don't doubt my damnation," I said. "But what is the point of this ritual? I can't find these people." When the captain didn't answer, I picked up one of the letters, glanced back at him, then unfolded it. The writing was hard to make out, as one might expect on a storm-tossed ship. At the end was a name: Stefan Blom. I glanced at other letters, from Martaan Willemssen, Bert Moorman. One was signed "Captain Hendrick Vanderdecken." I pointed and asked, "Is this you?"

"Read," he whispered.

It was addressed to his wife. The text began with rhetorical inquiries on her health and of their three children. He hoped the letter would reach her and that any correspondence she could write would reach him. From there, the narrative lurched into an account of misery, violence, and death, all counter to the current conditions where the crew toiled in perfunctory fashion. Apparently, the letter had been written some time ago as its author detailed the difficulties of passing through the Cape of Good Hope, on the other side of the world. A once dependable crew had turned mutinous over months of deprivation, and the captain had been forced to counter with draconian measures, executing two oft-whipped ringleaders. That and the scarcity of food and drinking water sapped the crew's rebelliousness. One by one they died. The survivors resorted to cannibalism. I found the subject matter repellent and thought it an odd letter to send to one's wife. I skipped to the end, and by the captain's name, I saw the date: October 27, 1682, nearly a hundred and forty years ago.

"I cannot deliver these," I said, "but I am grateful for you rescuing me. Is there any other way I can repay you?"

He gathered the letters and stuffed them into his jacket pocket.

"There is one here who does not belong. Only you can get him off," he said.

"You're talking about me? Once in sight of land, I will leave."

Vanderdecken turned away, our conversation over.

•   •   •

I made no friends in the following days. Everyone had a job and went through their paces. I tried to join in, but nothing I did made any impression. I ran a mop over the deck, but the dirt remained undisturbed. Torn sails fell apart moments after I sewed them. Someone always stood at the wheel and refused to allow me to take it. When I ascended to the crow's nest, I saw only clouds.

Captain Vanderdecken made no further attempts at communication. I wasn't anxious to fight the sea in my small craft again, but I knew I had to leave the ship soon for it contained no food or drink, and I had exhausted my own supply. I should have been ravenous, yet the ship had a narcotic effect, numbing my hunger. At night I chose an empty bunk and slept undisturbed. None of the crew ever slept.

On the fourth morning I climbed on deck and saw two spirits arguing with each other, though I couldn't hear their words, and perhaps none were spoken. One of the spirits had a pained look on his ravaged face but stood as if frozen. He held out a mop to the other spirit, whose wild brown hair shook in the wind like ribbons. The second spirit wanted nothing to do with the mop. It was the first sign of discord I'd seen on the ship. Curious, I approached, and the first spirit walked away. The second spirit looked at me in the face.

"Victor!" I said in disbelief.

He pulled at his stringy, unyielding hair. His face twisted before he spoke, as if he was straining to raise a monstrous fish that might devour him. "Even in death, I cannot avoid you. How did you survive the sea?"

"I don't know. I left Captain Walton's ship determined to destroy myself. But you were the source of my anger. With you gone, it seemed wrong to allow that anger to dictate what life remained to me."

"So, you took control. How arrogant."

"*Arrogant* is looking God in the face and thinking that you can do better."

He folded his arms, but they just went through each other. "I didn't look God in the face. I turned away, looked inside, and became intoxicated by dreams and desires. I rode that chariot, and like Phaethon, crashed and burned. Out of the ashes came you."

"I didn't ask to be born."

"No one does."

For the first time, I felt pity for him. Even a creator of life could be flawed—perhaps all creators. "So, your unrest has brought you here."

He shrugged. "It seems my restlessness is too great to be housed in heaven or hell. Or perhaps this is hell, when I stand face to face with the monster I created, but cannot destroy."

"You are more tormented than the other spirits here."

"They have had more time to accept nothingness."

"Shouldn't you do the same? What other choice have you?" I asked.

"I accept that I created a life that should not have been, and in doing so, stole lives meant for better things, including mine. What I don't accept is peace. If that can be granted to such as I, then all is a joke."

I thought about that, and of my own grappling. "Is it not the duty of all intelligent, creative men to venture into the unknown and attempt what lies beyond their power? Aren't we all doomed to fail? You didn't know this would happen."

"A murderer doesn't know he will become one."

His self-hatred had made him pathetic, and I recognized myself in him. My hands had killed. I had returned hate for hate, and it had brought me to the deck of a ghost ship.

"I cannot undo my sins, but I can learn from them," I said. "What if I return to the mainland, get to know people, and help them? That would lessen your crime."

His head rolled slightly. "Would you do that for me or yourself?"

"Both. Mostly for me."

"Then you'd better get off this ship."

He turned and vanished below deck.

•   •   •

The next morning a violent lurch woke me in my hammock. I staggered onto the deck and saw land in the distance. It was gray and desolate, offering a dare that most forms of life had spurned. Unlike my present circumstances, however, it had substance. Captain Vanderdecken appeared next to me and stuffed his letters into my shirt. Some spirits never give up. We lowered my weather-beaten boat into the sea, and I paddled. The farther I got from the ship, the harder I rowed, until my craft scraped onto the shore, and I fell onto the sand. Remembering my benefactors, I turned around and watched the ship fade into mist. I later learned I had reached a deserted island in the Spitsbergen archipelago. Though I found no human beings, I did locate the ruins of a fort. From that I patched up my boat as best I could. With my knife I killed an ailing reindeer. Other wildlife, such as an occasional polar bear, arctic foxes, ptarmigans, and an auk passed me with impunity.

I was reticent to again trade solid ground for the dangers of the ocean but changed my mind on the fifth day when another ship came into view. It was about two miles away. I paddled my boat toward it as if my life depended on it.

It was a Russian whaler. When the crew hauled me in, they weren't sure whether to offer me shelter, throw me back in, or harpoon me. The only Russian word I knew was "nyet," which wouldn't open many doors. By now my extended time at sea had made my frightful appearance appropriate.

Plenty of use was found for my brute strength, such as swabbing the deck and pulling in whale carcasses, but my errant tosses soon excluded me from harpoon activity. My lack of Russian kept me separated from the crew, but the captain, a burly, red-faced man named Konstantin Dryomov, knew quite a bit of German. As I was the only other educated person on board, he took an interest in me. He reminded me of the blind man I had befriended. Once we got to know each other, it became our habit to discuss the great philosophical questions, particularly how they pertained to whaling.

"Whales, they have big objection to being killed. They have big everything," he said to me one evening on the deck, the salty air absorbing his pipe smoke.

"How did you get into the whaling business?" I asked.

"One day I wake up and was whaler."

"Really? You just decided that's what you wanted to do?"

"No." He frowned. "I wake up from drinking more vodka than possible and find I be shanghaied onto whaling ship. I tell captain I want off. He say, 'We drop you off next stop.' It take two years."

"If you didn't like whaling, why didn't you leave the profession?"

"Was my plan. But we arrive Vladivostok, my pockets full of money and my head with dreams. My mates insist we celebrate at inn, but I say this first day of rest of life. I go alone. I walk Vladivostok's streets past its gray, broke houses, and think, *Goodbye, whales.* After hours of steps, I chose my inn. *White Cliffs* on your language. I draw crowd with my whaling stories, only little bit lies. Listeners keep my tankard full. Next I know, it late morning and I half-dressed on bed, head exploding, pockets empty. Only thing I can afford is kick flying me into street. Sailing all I know. In days, I sign on another whaler." He took another puff. "If not for whales, my life be very different. So, I declare war on them. Not free until every one harpooned."

"Shouldn't you blame the whalers? It's not the whales' fault there is a whaling trade."

"Life not fair, for people or whales."

Determined to interact more with the former, I did my work and tolerated flat head jokes. My education and proximity to the captain made me unpopular with the crew, however. A turning point came when Captain Dryomov discovered a barrel of wine was missing. As watered-down wine was the principal drink of the sailors and was used to disinfect drinking water, this was not an insignificant theft. The cook was accused, but he vowed his innocence. As the cook had treated me fairly, if not warmly, I decided to look into it.

I kept an eye on the sailors, trying to spot one who was drunk at an inexplicable time, but most of these men were heavy drinkers who could hold copious amounts of alcohol without showing it. There weren't that many places to hide something as large as a barrel. The most cluttered place was the hold where the whale oil was kept in 35-gallon barrels, of which we had nearly a hundred filled ones at the time. As these were larger than the keg of wine, the oil barrels would make a good hiding place. The thing was, the filled barrels were nailed shut and wouldn't be easy for the thief to reopen. As I was leaving the hold, I ran into the carpenter, a sallow, taciturn sailor named Krupin. He acted as if he'd forgotten something and turned around. Later, I asked the captain why Krupin would be in the hold. Dryomov said he was in there often, as he built the oil barrels. I said, if the keg is hidden in one of the barrels, a likely culprit would be the one that made them. As we weren't about to open a hundred nailed barrels, we needed to keep an eye on Krupin.

Krupin may have suspected something and kept away from the hold for two days. On the third, he got careless, and I followed him in. He approached one of the barrels, on which he'd hidden a hinge that opened the top. As he filled his mug, I confronted him. He considered my superior size, then backed down, opting for five lashes rather than my fists. Dryomov thanked me and suggested I be a detective for a living. I laughed. Other than the captain, whose job it was to deal with hardened men, who would trust a monster like me to find things they'd lost? On further reflection, however, I thought, what was a monster but someone who couldn't channel his negative qualities? Could I turn being a monster into a strength? I was educated, strong, and had insight into the extremes of human nature. I could bill myself: *Frankenstein, No Case Too Monstrous*, if I could ever get to dry land.

One night while we were standing on deck, looking over a flat sea, I confided to the captain my thoughts about a second chance. "Whatever I do, it needs to be something I can justify. People either make the world better or worse. So far, I've done only the second one."

Dryomov took a puff on his ever-present pipe. "Find your strengths and make up for your sins. If not, you wake up on a whaler."

Or on Captain Walton's ship, *The Flying Dutchman*, or a tiny craft on a dangerous sea.

A month later, Captain Dryomov dropped me off in Christiania, Norway. I had a little money and a lot of desire to stay on land. The captain had more money, and I asked him to come with me and start a new life.

He laughed and patted my broad shoulder.

"If I come, I not be me. But you, I have faith."

I chuckled. "You're the only one."

But as it turned out, he wasn't. Alone again, in a simple inn, by the light of a fire, I took another look at the letters given to me by Captain Vanderdecken. The sending addresses were mostly but not all in Holland. One was France, another England, and a third, Algeria. A final piece of paper appeared newer than the rest. To my astonishment, I saw the name "Monster" on it, with a Geneva address. Under it were the words: "Redeem me, and yourself." It was signed "Victor Frankenstein."

2

The Monster is the Father to the Child

"**A**RE YOU FRANKENSTEIN?"

The question was laughable. I was seven feet tall, with a head flatter than the Netherlands, and twin electrodes sticking out the sides of my neck. I was either Frankenstein or the latest in Halloween shoe trees. After returning to Geneva from a two-year exile in the Arctic—a hideout I'd recommend to anyone while the heat was on—I'd opened a detective agency. With some fanfare, I'd adopted the name of Frankenstein. Victor, being dead, didn't need it anymore, it beat the hell out of "monster", and it was what most people wanted to call me anyway.

"That's me. What can I do for you?"

I took one look at this twitching middle-aged man and guessed he was missing most of what makes life worth living: self-esteem, confidence, love, and security. I could only hope he wasn't going to hire me to find all those things.

"Your name is associated with … other monsters. No offense."

This was another case of my reputation doing my work for me. I didn't actually socialize with the Wolfman, the Creature from the Black Lagoon, or the Mummy, but it didn't hurt to allow people to think I had such contacts. Being a monster myself gave me a certain insight.

"None taken. What's your problem?"

The bluntness of my question caused him to fall apart, as if he were the Incredible Melting Man. "I think a vampire is attacking my daughter," he said, blubbering. He landed in my chair, glancing off the raised arm. I waited for him to reconstitute himself, then asked for details. He spoke in a deliberate voice.

"My name is Christof Heinzmann. I own a public house called the Kronnenhall. My daughter Alessia, until recently, worked there as a barmaid. She was popular with the customers and fairly responsible for a 19-year-old. But in the past month, she has been too weak to get out of her bed."

"So, she spends all her time inside."

Heinzmann sat up. "No! She vanishes at night. Every evening I sit in her room but, you know how vampires are, they have that ability to make you fall asleep. When I wake up, Alessia is gone. She always returns just before dawn, but I can never get her to tell me where she's been."

She sounded like a normal teenager to me. "She doesn't say anything?"

"Just that she couldn't sleep and needed to go for a walk."

This had Dracula's teeth all over it. I told Heinzmann I'd take his case.

Dracula and I weren't friends. For one thing, we kept different hours. He liked to burn the midnight oil, while I tended to get cranky if I wasn't shaking hands with the sandman by 10:30 p.m. We both liked young people, but whereas I liked to pat them on the head, he liked to bite them on the neck. He also had a horrible accent. I'd worked really hard with a speech therapist to transform my "arrghs" and "rowlls" into standard English—no one was going to hire someone who sounded like a junkyard dog—but Dracula still never met a "w" that didn't knock him for a loop.

I didn't know where he laid out his coffin these days, but that didn't matter. There was a sad predictability about Dracula. All I had to do was sit up in Alessia's bedroom and wait. Around 7 p.m. I strolled into a coffeehouse and downed enough coffee to animate a corpse. I then reported to the Heinzmann house, carefully noting the location of the bathroom. Though I'd put on a tie and Heinzmann introduced me, his wife, a plump long-haired woman, hit the ceiling. After we scraped her off, Heinzmann led me to his daughter's bedroom.

It was like stepping into a gothic castle. The walls and the drawn window curtains had been painted black. A rusty pair of handcuffs sat on top of a small dresser. Portraits of grim, sallow-faced men and women stared at me, as if criticizing the fact that I was alive. I motioned toward them.

"Are those ancestors?"

Heinzmann shrugged. "I don't know who they are. I just know they're creepy."

The reverence for death in this room was palpable. I used to be dead, and let me tell you, it's nothing to write home about. As a matter of fact, it's nothing *period*. The other thing I didn't get was how gothic worshippers went to great pains to be like monsters. I'm a monster and not proud of it. Why would anyone want to add to the pain and misery in this world?

In the twilight I saw the sleeping figure of Alessia, her black sheet half covering her tiny body. Youth had left her pretty, but she was all skin and bones. This was just the way Dracula liked them, except she had a high metal content, her body liberally pierced with rings. Her dyed black hair and black lipstick contrasted with her pale face.

I turned to Heinzmann. "Did you tell her I was sitting with her tonight?"

He grasped his hands together. "Yes, but she never listens to anything I say. It doesn't matter. She won't wake up until she is about to leave."

"All right. You two get a good night's sleep. By morning we'll know more."

Heinzmann retreated to his bedroom. Behind a closed door I thought I heard Mrs. Heinzmann say, "I'm supposed to sleep with *him* in my house?"

In the corner of Alessia's room was a wooden rocking chair that went with the rest of the room like a baby carriage in a funeral home. Figuring Heinzmann had put it there for my use, I sat down and, for one of the few times in my life, I rocked. The pendulum of a cuckoo clock ticked hypnotically. With all the caffeine in my system, I wasn't worried about falling sleep—I was more worried about ever falling asleep again. Nor did Dracula frighten me. He liked his necks about a third the circumference of mine.

A short interval after the cuckoo sounded twelve times, I heard a tapping on the window. It was softer than my rocking, yet somehow Alessia stirred. In a trance she rose to her feet and opened the window lock. Silhouetted by the moon, a six-foot tall man in a cape stepped into the room. Alessia fell into his arms. To my disgust I heard a soft growling, as Dracula opened his mouth wider than any human.

"You really do have a way with women," I said.

The vampire let go of Alessia, who crumpled to the floor. "Whoooo's theeeeeer?" he asked. A speech therapist wouldn't know where to start with him.

I rose to my full height. "Frankenstein, private detective. I cannot allow you to take this innocent girl."

He laughed. "You haff ze wrong guurl. Zare is no-thing innnnocent abooooout hurr." From this point, I will dispense with the dialect, which was nearly as irritating to listen to as to spell.

"Be that as it may, you have no right to her."

"Hmm. I'm sure I don't have to explain my needs to you."

"I'm not interested."

"I wouldn't expect interest from a monster formed by the unnatural union of a diseased mind and a revived dead body. Do you even know whose rest was disturbed so that you might live?"

"No, and it's irrelevant." Had Victor not unearthed this body, it would have decomposed long ago. Its former owner was not affected. Be that as it may, I had no desire to match monster ethics with a vampire.

Dracula ran his claw-like hand through his hair. I noticed we both had that plastered-to-the-skull look. "Do you plan to spend the remaining evenings of this girl's life rocking in her bedroom?" he asked. "Time means nothing to me. I will be back."

He climbed out the window. I couldn't fit so I rushed to the door and chased after him. He laughed, transformed into a bat, and flew away. I retreated to the bedroom and laid Alessia onto her bed. I then shut and locked the window and resumed my rocking chair vigil. The rest of the night proved uneventful.

In the morning I gave the Heinzmanns my report.

"If Dracula wants my daughter," Heinzmann said, "how can we stop him?"

"Leave that to me," I said, sounding more confident than I felt.

The truth was I needed help. My large size and lumbering gait made it difficult to tail anyone clandestinely. Besides the pyramids and the Great Wall of China, there were few landscapes I blended into. I needed to hire someone small, loyal, and desperate for money. Igor, Victor's former servant, was the man for me.

I asked around the city bars and was pointed towards a depressing basement flat, a far cry from his Frankenstein castle days. The lock on his door was broken, and I found him passed out, his head lying on the tabletop. In that position, the summit of his body was his hunchback. He slobbered several oaths as I roused him.

"What are you doing here?" he snarled.

The ceiling was low, and I had to bend my head. His bed offered the only other seating option. I pointed to it. "Do you mind?"

He sighed. "Go ahead. I don't usually get that far anyway."

I sat with the mattress protesting. "I need your help."

"Ha! Why should I help you? You killed my master!"

"I didn't kill him. The Arctic did. I didn't ask him to chase me up there." After I said that, Igor's harsh features softened. We had one thing in common. I didn't ask to be born a monster, and Igor didn't ask to be built like a camel.

"I'm not so good at helping myself," he said finally. "What makes you think I can help you?"

I explained I needed someone unexpected to follow Dracula to his home. He chuckled weakly at the vampire's name, as if his life revolved from one monster to another. Sensing his interest waning, I laid it on about how one way we as monsters could redeem ourselves was protecting the innocence of others.

"And you'll pay me for this, beforehand?" he asked.

"Name your sum."

"A thousand florins."

I grimaced. "Now name a sum that you have some hope of getting."

"You just want me to follow him to his home?"

"That's it."

"Because if he attacks me, I don't think the world is ready for a hunchbacked vampire."

"Just find out where he lives."

He leaned his chin on his fist, giving the appearance of deep thought. "I could do it for ten. "

"Done."

For the next couple of nights Igor hid in the bushes outside the Heinzmann home, while I sat in Alessia's bedroom. Despite what I said about Dracula being predictable, he didn't show up. During the day I noticed, for apparently the first time in weeks, Alessia showing some color besides white skin and black clothes. She also showed ill-temper, ridiculing my appearance and adding, "As a sleep aid, you're a real zero." Heinzmann made excuses for her, but it was unnecessary. I recognized vampire withdrawal when I saw it.

"Maybe you scared Dracula off," Heinzmann said hopefully, but I knew that wasn't the case. Living for hundreds of years,

Dracula had a different perspective. What could I threaten him with? A stake in the heart? I would have been doing him a favor. He was in a perfect position to just bide his time.

On the third night I learned a woman was attacked on the street near Lake Geneva. The victim was young, attractive, with no memory of her assailant. If she didn't have two cut marks on her neck, I'd eat my smoking jacket. Had my interest in Alessia caused him to hunt elsewhere? I received an answer two mornings later, standing in my doorway.

"Our boy was prowling in the bushes outside the Heinzmann house last night," Igor said importantly. "You're not going to believe this, but I followed him to the basement of St. Paul's Church."

"That's impossible. He can't stand in the presence of a cross."

"Perhaps not, but that's where he went. There's a side entrance to the basement. Maybe he closed his eyes when he got close to the cross."

The more I thought about it, the more brilliant it seemed. Nobody would look for Dracula in the basement of a church. Nobody except me.

That evening when the lid of Dracula's coffin rose, I was surprised by several things that didn't happen. I didn't hear the screech of rusty hinges turning, nor did Dracula show alarm when he saw me standing in front of him like a hanging judge. His bushy eyebrows merely lowered, and he scowled. "I've woken up to worse."

"Nice place," I said. The basement was dusty, dark, and cluttered, a repository for broken furniture, cracked vases, and unwanted paintings.

He stiffened, and he was already stiff. "I am used to more ostentatious housing but, in truth, my wants are simple."

"What's it like to hear a sermon and discover you're the subject?"

"Thankfully, there is no activity at this church during my active hours. Besides, I'm sure there's no shortage of devout churchgoers who find themselves in the reverend's sermons."

Dracula enjoyed verbal jousting, but I found it tedious. "Your attacks on Alessia Heinzmann end here."

He frowned. "I haven't touched her in nearly a week."

"That's because I've been sitting in her bedroom. You would have touched her last night."

He climbed out of the coffin, shut it, and sat on top of it, looking more like a transient than a caped aristocrat. "I choose my contacts carefully. People call me unnatural, yet this girl is merely following her inclinations. You spent time in her room. I didn't put those paintings on that black wall. She was worshipping death before I met her. I am helping her move toward self-actualization."

I hated the sound of my laugh, which resembled a wave of groans, but I couldn't help myself. "How is it self-actualization to drain a human body of its blood? The self is you."

"I'm talking about her. Alessia is self-destructive. The other night by Lake Geneva I found a substitute for her, but she'll just as certainly find a substitute for me. To escape her clueless parents and immature peers, she'll turn to alcohol, drugs, and abusive sex."

"You don't know that."

"I've lived for hundreds of years. I do know that. But ..." He raised his bony white hand. "I give you my word I will leave her alone."

"What good is your word? Do you cross your heart and hope to die? There's only one way to end this." I patted a box I had placed on the floor. "You know my philosophy. Speak softly and carry a hawthorn stake."

Dracula laughed mirthlessly. "You brought your tools, did you? Good. This place could use some touching up." I felt his icy breath as his eyes bore down on me. "Do you think I'm so stupid that at dawn, I'll saunter back here, lay down, and let you play *Pin the stake in the vampire*? Do you think I've lived this long with only one coffin? I have a coffin in every port!"

"I'm sure you do," I said, clamping my ape-like right hand onto his arm. "But that doesn't matter if you can't get to it."

He struggled, but for once we were playing to my strength. He turned into a bat, flapping his bony wings like a storm-ravaged sail, but I just tightened my grip. As I held him at arm's length, his claws could rake only the air. He grew limp, then reassumed human form.

"So, you're just going to hold onto me for ten hours?" he asked.

"I have nowhere else to be."

He nodded. "That's your tragedy."

We sat on top of his coffin. The hours passed slowly as the muscles in my right arm throbbed. I thought about my sins: the deaths of my master's beloved Elizabeth and, indirectly, Victor himself. At least I'd tried to tame the monster within me, while Dracula had accommodated his. Destroying him was a small step toward my redemption. I suggested he reflect on his centuries of crime. He said everyone knew vampires couldn't reflect.

Then I saw angels, or perhaps birds. It wasn't very clear.

Just before that, in the corner of my eye. I saw Alessia, wielding my own hammer in the direction of my skull.

I woke up alone with an empty coffin and, incredibly, a flatter head than I'd started the evening with. I put two and two together and got nothing. Apparently, despite a week's lapse in their physical relationship, Dracula still had some power over Alessia. He'd sent her a telepathic message: *Come to the church and free me. Blunt object provided.*

With that turn of events, you might think they lived miserably ever after, but no. Dracula shipped out to parts unknown, leaving Alessia to self-actualize without him. Figuring I owed it to my employer, I kept an eye on her. She wasted no time filling in the void, frequenting the most disreputable taverns at all hours, engaging in sordid activity I haven't the stomach to describe. She even dated Igor a couple of times. She must have noticed me tailing her, but she never told me to leave or even acknowledged my presence. As she stumbled home on the last night, I broke the silence.

"Alessia," I said. "I know you can hear me following you." The clump of my boat-sized feet left a wake of open window blinds. "I need to say one thing."

She halted so abruptly that I almost ran her over. "You made him leave!" she hissed. Her eyes were as brilliant and unfocused as a Turner painting.

"He didn't care about you."

"He made me feel good."

"He created a need that he satisfied temporarily." I grabbed her shoulders. She cringed but didn't fight me. "Listen now and remember later. There is an attraction to being a monster. You mistake the ability to destroy, to break the rules, to hurt, as power to wield against disappointment and pain. It's less of a weapon and more of a disease, however. You reduce your world to a wasteland and yourself to waste. At some point we all tire of being monsters."

She laughed in my face, long, full, and final.

I *didn't* have a way with women.

The next day I visited the Heinzmanns. In view of Alessia's continued downward path, I offered to forfeit my fee. Heinzmann insisted on paying, however, as I had successfully removed Dracula. I urged both parents to remain open and available to their daughter.

Later, I wrote up some notes in my office. I thought of the long, winding path that brought me here. The prospect of closure had drawn me to the detective field. Unfortunately, while some cases are open and shut, others are like a creaking door whose sound you can't get out of your head. Even with Dracula out of the picture, I knew the root of Alessia's problem still flowed in her blood. I promised myself I would check on her from time to time.

When I next looked up, a heavy-set middle-aged woman stood in the doorway. Her gloved hands clasped tightly to a faded purse.

"Are you Frankenstein?" she asked.

The question seemed more pertinent now.

"I am."

3

Before the Beginning

WITH NO CASES PENDING, I spent a frustrating morning shopping for a hat. My head, with its large size and singular flatness, begs cover yet confounds the most ambitious milliner. When put to the test, each of my selections perched precariously, either pulled down over my eyes or tilted up in the style of a country rube. None would resist a brisk wind, so I departed unadorned and *au natural*, or at least as much as possible, being the monster of Victor Frankenstein.

Entering my office, I spotted a smudged piece of paper on the floor. Releasing its uneven folds, I read the following: "SEE YOU AT 11." It was already 11:30. Despite the limited number of characters, three mistakes were crossed out. I glanced out the window at Geneva's bustling streets. A horse cart clattered by; a beggar accosted an impatient, well-dressed man; and a mother dragged her protesting child to the other side of the street. Though mine was a specialized practice, I'd recently advertised heavily in the newspapers. Certainly, someone out there had a problem I could solve.

"Mr. Frankenstein."

A man of below average height with a triangular mustache and black, curly hair stood in my doorway. His frayed, dark clothes spoke of a good past and a bleak future. His flattened nose suggested an encounter with a rock or a hard place. He smelled like a dead animal.

"Frankenstein will do. Are you the author of the note left under my door?"

"I am. My name is Hamlin Baudry." His right hand shook slightly. "Does that mean anything to you?"

It didn't, yet there was a frustrated, downtrodden neediness about him that I found all too familiar.

"Sorry. There are many people in the city I don't know." He nodded and seemed relieved. "Have a seat and tell me how I can be of assistance."

Baudry sat cautiously, as if he didn't always have the option of a chair. Clients usually find me intimidating on first sight, but Hamlin possessed either a tougher constitution or had seen me before, treating me as if everyone stood seven feet tall with electrodes protruding from their neck.

"I'm told you are good at what you do," he said.

"My past is such that I have to be good. If you want something found, I will not give up until I find it."

"Of course." He stared at the floor, and I became self-conscious of the three cracked tiles I needed to replace. Finally, his eyes still averted, he resumed talking. "Do you work alone?"

I wondered when he would get to the point. "No one in this business works entirely alone and succeeds. Sometimes a man from my days at the Frankenstein castle helps me." He didn't look happy about that so I added, "It doesn't affect my fee."

He nodded. "I don't imagine you're welcome at that castle."

"No. I haven't been there since the death of my creator. Mr. Baudry, if you would just tell me what I can do for you, I'm sure ..."

But before I could finish, he abruptly stood, his head of curly hair lurching unnaturally to the left. He was wearing a wig.

"I'm afraid I've changed my mind."

"Are you sure? I ..." but he was already out the door. Puzzled and disappointed, I stood at the window and watched him vanish into the milling crowds. Why would he come twice, ask me some personal questions, and then leave? Did he wear an ill-fitting wig to hide his baldness or his identity? How had my short answers made him decide against hiring me? Clearly, something was bothering him. Had I been a busier man, I would have left it at that. But I have much to make up for, and after an uneventful hour, I decided to investigate on my own.

•   •   •

As a detective, I found the City Hall's Department of Records a useful resource but never liked the place. The ventilation was poor, and the short, mustachioed clerk hated tall people. As I walked into the main office, he sat perched on a high stool behind a cluttered desk, his bespectacled eyes glued on the pages of a thick book. He groaned when I asked if he could fetch me the latest register of people living in Geneva.

"Aren't you here to serve me?" I asked, as he returned from the basement and handed me the book, which I took to an uneven table.

"Apparently," he grunted.

I found twenty Baudrys listed but no Hamlins. Either he was from out of town, or his name was as false as his wig. At the risk of further perturbing the man on the high stool, I requested the register from ten years earlier. I thumbed through the dusty pages and there he was: Hamlin Baudry. He lived on Rue du Bouie with his mother, Berthe. I rechecked the current listing and found Berthe, though at a different address.

•   •   •

Berthe Baudry lived in a basement flat. A primitive sign above rotted wooden steps said "Berthe's Laundry and Sewing," though her penmanship outclassed her son's in every way. She saw me hesitate at the steps.

"No!" she exclaimed. "I do alternations, but there's a limit."

"Madame Baudry?"

"Madame Sauvage handles oversized men." Her eyes lit on my flat skull. "What happened to your head?"

"A birth defect. I've been looking for a hat to cover it, but as you implied, my size is problematic. At any rate, it is not your ability as a seamstress that brings me here. I'd like to talk to your son, Hamlin."

Her face clouded and her eyes moistened. "Why?"

"I'm a detective. He came to my office this morning. At first, he seemed anxious to see me, but then suddenly he just left." She looked at me as I'd suggested arsenic be used as a coffee additive. "Perhaps I'm wasting my time—"

"Hamlin has been dead for four years," she said, her voice cracking.

Confused, I described the man.

"I've never seen him in a wig, but otherwise that could be Andre, my good for nothing brother-in-law," Berthe said. "I have no idea why he'd want a detective. Usually, it's the law and landlords that are looking for *him*."

In a torrent of words, she told me Andre was the shame of the family, a cruel, unpredictable man who could never hold a job and spent whatever money he had on alcohol. She had no idea where he lived these days and added, "He probably doesn't either." Nor did she know why he would pretend to be her son.

"How did Hamlin die?"

The woman's fleshy arms fluttered then flopped to her sides. "Four years ago, he never came home from work. The next day I received a note from him saying he was sorry but had to leave for a while. Later that day I learned his employer had been robbed in the night."

"But you say he's dead."

"Hamlin was a blacksmith's apprentice. He would not have robbed his employer, and he would never have left me."

"Were you in need of money at the time?"

"Of course. And after Hamlin disappeared, I had to move to this place." She waved dismissively at her house. "But Hamlin was not a thief. He had plans. If you want a case, you should find out what happened to him."

"What kind of a relationship did Hamlin have with Andre?"

She sighed. "No one is close to Andre. Not even Andre. If the human body didn't need food and shelter, I'd never see him, which would be fine with me."

I stared at this tiny woman whose life had been turned upside-down by tragedy. The Romantic poets could write pages of the nurturing sea, healing trees and singing birds. Reality resembled more an implacable stone and a desolate mountain. Since I'd returned from my exile in the Arctic, I'd made it my job to bridge the gap.

"Do you know the name and address of the blacksmith?"

•   •   •

The next day I paid a visit to Franz Koehler at his small property on the northern edge of the city. The metallic odor and smoke of heated iron assaulted my nostrils as I entered his back yard. Koehler stood over a table, banging out a future pair of horseshoes. His bulging biceps argued for the iron's submission. I'd informed him of my visit and its reasons by afternoon post, so no surprise showed on his bearded face as I entered.

"You must be Frankenstein," he said in a voice of gravel and phlegm.

"And you, Franz Koehler, former employer of Hamlin Baudry."

He looked at me with suspicion. "I am. Why are you asking about Hamlin Baudry?"

"Have you ever met his mother or uncle?"

"No, but I hear his mother does capable sewing work and that his uncle does no work at all. Hamlin did all I asked of him. He would have been a good blacksmith."

"He had ability?"

"That, and patience, maturity, and a willingness to learn."

He shook his head. "The last day I saw him, four years ago now, he robbed me. If he'd asked, I would have lent him the money."

"How much did he steal?"

"Nearly two hundred florins."

"What do you think happened to him?" I asked.

Koehler kneaded his expansive forehead. "I've given that much thought. He wasn't used to money. Maybe after he stole it, he let it be seen, and someone killed him for it."

The next step was to find out why Andre Baudry had pretended to be Hamlin. Unfortunately, despite his infamy, no one knew where he lived. I asked around, but the clearest answer I got was, "Where he falls." More often than not, that was in the poorest areas of Geneva. I decided to consult my specialist.

I found Igor where I usually did, sprawled out on his floor in his flat.

I gently roused him. "I don't know why you ever invested in a bed."

"Sometimes I have guests," he growled, "who, unlike you, have the decency to come only when I pay."

"Ever hear of Andre Baudry?"

He turned onto his side and gagged. "Heard, seen, and smelled. I may have brushed up against him as well, but that might have just been a nightmare."

"When did you encounter him?"

"Baudry was a grave robber. Victor needed bodies for his experiments but wanted nothing to do with Baudry, who had a terrible reputation. Part of my job was to keep him away."

"Were you successful?"

"Yes. I had principles then. Victor was noble, brilliant, self-sacrificing. Baudry was the opposite. They needed to stay apart. He never gave up though. Even a year after Victor died and I was still caretaker of the castle, I saw Baudry lurking outside the gate, as if he was hoping I'd buy his dead bodies. What do you care about him?"

I described Baudry's visit to my office and how I was now looking into the death of Hamlin.

Igor bellowed a ghoulish laugh that seemed to shake his vital organs against the bars of his ribs. "You're lucky Baudry didn't hire you. He and money don't go together."

"I have some questions for him. From what I've heard, you two frequent the same low roads." I pressed a fistful of florins into Igor's hand. He stared at them thoughtfully, then kissed them.

Next, I stopped at the police station to see what they had on Hamlin's disappearance, which turned out to be no more than I already knew. They had a lot more on Andre, who'd been arrested for vagrancy, public disturbance, and twice for grave robbing, most recently four months ago.

•   •   •

I returned to my third floor flat, heated up some leftover sauerkraut and washed it down with murky beer. Sometimes the combination inspired me. Baudry had pretended to be Hamlin and asked if I'd ever heard of him, if I worked alone, and if I frequented the Frankenstein castle. Why did he care? According to Igor, Baudry had badgered Victor to buy his wares. What if Victor had relented? What if Andre killed his own nephew and sold it to Victor? A ghastly thought roiled my senses. I was the product of dead bodies, and Hamlin disappeared in 1792, the same year I was created. What if a part of Hamlin lived in me?

Early the next morning I checked on Igor. After cursing at me for waking him up, he muttered that he'd tracked down several of Baudry's unpaid bar bills but hadn't caught up with him yet. "Hope you don't mind, but I've hired myself out to two of the tavern owners."

"I've always encouraged you to improve yourself."

"One of the owners thought Baudry was still involved in body snatching, and there is a burial scheduled for tomorrow afternoon. He thought Baudry was a good bet to dig up the body tomorrow night."

"Lots of people die," I said. "Does Baudry dig up every one?"

"No, but the deceased was young. He drowned in the river. He'd be a perfect specimen."

We agreed to meet at the cemetery at dusk. In the meantime, I decided I needed to visit a place I'd avoided since my return to Geneva.

•　　　•　　　•

Seeing Victor's boarded-up castle again reminded me of a caged phoenix. Inside its walls Victor had dreamed of becoming a benevolent God who ushered in a new dawn, but his audacious reach had resulted in something he could never grasp: me.

Outside I walked to the back of the room where I was created and saw the corrosion on the window's metal mesh. It stood twenty feet off the ground, but under it lay a storage shed. I clambered onto its sagging roof, and with a grunt, yanked the metal mesh free.

Tangled wires still lined the walls and ceiling as if spun by a monstrous, metallic spider. Dust covered a network of pipes, wheels, and levers that only Victor could comprehend. Angular lightning conductors pointed toward the sky. In the center sat the long, narrow table where I was made, the restraints hanging like broken arms after I'd escaped.

As Victor believed his every thought and deed worthy of preservation, he would have recorded a transaction with a body snatcher. The lab was his office, sanctuary, and prison, and in a far corner I found what I was looking for: a bookcase with his writings. Diaries, poetry, and experiments all lay untouched, as no one wanted to walk down Victor's road. You might think it strange I didn't seek these notebooks earlier. In response, I would ask, if you had access to the private thoughts of your creator, would you want to know them? I had more than enough information to fuel my shame.

I found Victor's book of financial transactions buried in a bottom shelf. I flipped through the yellowed pages. Every electrode, gear, and scalpel were listed, including the seller and the price paid. A day before I took my first breath was this entry: "30 florins, organic materials, AB." There it was. Victor had done business with Andre Baudry, and chances were, as he was obsessed with only one experiment at the time, the organic materials were likely used in my creation. Igor once asked me if I felt guilt that others died so I could live. I responded that those unfortunates were already dead. But what if Andre killed his nephew for the express purpose of selling him to Victor? Had I not been created, Hamlin might have raised a happy family. I closed the notebook and stuck it back in its place, but its contents stayed inside me.

•　　•　　•

I hid behind an enormous statue of a rich businessman's dead wife. A crescent moon poked in and out from behind drifting clouds. Oblong headstones appeared and vanished under the intermittent light. A fitful breeze moaned snatches of a broken song. Normally, this was my favorite time of day, dark and quiet enough to escape the evidence of sight or mind. Not tonight, though. I was worried that Igor was late, but then I heard scuffling footsteps approaching me from behind.

"Nice night for robbing a grave," I said, turning around. It wasn't Igor.

"Don't move," a familiar voice said. Baudry, now bald without his wig, stuck a knife under my chin. His left eye was puffy and his torn shirt splattered with blood.

"Cut yourself?"

"Igor did, though I suspect most of the blood is his."

"Where is he?"

"He is no more. I cracked his head open with my shovel. I should have killed that camel years ago, but I let it go because no listened to him. Then I saw your advertisement.

You hadn't died in the Arctic. I had to know what you knew about Hamlin."

Had I caused the death of yet another person close to me? It was too terrible to consider.

"I didn't know anything."

"That was clear from our meeting, but then I found out the hunchback was asking questions and following me around. Why would he suddenly do that unless you'd discovered my secret. So, I got the owner of Le Baron Rouge to point him in the direction of this cemetery."

"Igor didn't know anything about you and Hamlin either. If you'd just stayed away, we would never have known."

Baudry shook his head. "You're a detective. I couldn't take that chance."

So he had taken Igor's life, and he was going to take mine unless I could stop him.

"What I don't understand is how can you kill your own nephew and sell his body to a mad scientist?"

He smiled without joy. "Hamlin threatened to report my bodysnatching to the police. I needed to convince him otherwise, but I wasn't welcome at his house, so we met as he was leaving the blacksmith's. The argument got heated, and … he accidentally hit his head against a concrete wall."

"Did you steal the two hundred florins he had in his pocket?"

"He never had two hundred florins in his pocket. Unbeknownst to my sister-in-law, Hamlin liked to join me in an occasional drink at the pub after work. He let slip the location of his employer's savings. I stole it later that night to make it look as if Hamlin had the money to run off." He laughed, a hollow sound, as a drop of blood welled above his eye. "You and I have two things in common."

"What's that?"

"Hamlin was the first person I killed. He made me what I am today. Just like he's a part of you."

"What's the other thing?" I asked.

His eyes settled on me. "We've both killed."

I couldn't justify myself, but I had to keep him talking. "We can't change that. What's important now is the present and future."

"Yes, and I will have neither if I'm arrested for the murder of Hamlin."

Time stood still, and I thought how ironic it was that the two people responsible for my life, Victor and Baudry, both wanted me dead. Then a shovel clanged on top of Baudry's skull, dropping him senseless to the ground. Igor laid the shovel next to him. "You shouldn't leave shovels in the woods where camels can find them."

I stared at Igor, dazed. "I thought you were dead."

"So did he. His shovel glanced off my hump, absorbing most of the impact. I guess it's good for something."

He had blood on his head and back, so I resisted the urge to embrace him.

While Igor stood guard on our captive, I rousted a farmer and borrowed his horse cart so I could take Igor to the hospital and Baudry to the police station. Baudry never admitted to the murder of Hamlin, and Victor's account book wasn't enough to convict him. He was wrong about Igor though. A jury did listen to him, and Baudry got five years for attempted murder.

Before the trial, I visited Berthe, revealing Andre's confession to Hamlin's murder and theft of the blacksmith's money. She'd always suspected the truth but feared her brother-in-law. She could not afford to pay me but promised a lifetime of free sewing services. Certain it would not give her solace, I did not reveal my connection to her son. I didn't even know what parts of him, if any, lived on in me. I could only try to honor his unfulfilled life with mine.

The last time I saw Berthe was in my office, after the trial. Looking humble but unbowed, she handed me a sack.

"Please accept this. It's outside my area of expertise, but it could help when you feel the need to fit into a crowd."

From the sack I pulled out the largest flat cap I'd ever seen.

4

Voodoo as I Say

ONE MORNING A DARK-HAIRED WOMAN in her mid-twenties walked into my office. A flowing blue dress hung on her small frame, while her gaunt face hid under a wide hat containing enough feathers for flight. A fraying at her elbows suggested her blouse had been in the family a while. Her pale lips fluttered. In respect, I rose to my full seven-foot height, and then she spoke.

"My husband is a zombie."

Gallows humor comes naturally to consulting detectives, and even more so to products of unnatural science, such as myself, but I resisted answering, *I am the monster of Frankenstein. How do you do?* Or, *who introduced you to each other? The Wolf-man?* Instead, I just said, "Please, have a seat and tell me more." She sank into one of my two client chairs, and I reassumed mine.

"My name is Ada Kurzmann. My husband Hrolf is a good, hardworking man, but he has no patience for perceived slights. We live next door to Perodin Orchards. Have you heard of it?"

"I have." The sprawling orchard, located on the northwestern outskirts of Geneva, was the source of nasty rumors: its owner abused his workers, many of whom he imported from his ancestral home in Haiti. Most people still bought his apples, however.

"We've long considered moving because some nights the most heartbreaking screams and moans come from that orchard," she continued.

"Were you able to make out any actual words?" I asked.

"They were not in a language we understood, but there was no mistaking the pain in those utterances. Last week Hrolf went to the police. They said they'd pay Perodin a visit first thing in the morning, but two nights later, we heard the screams again. On the third night, Wednesday, my husband said he would put a stop to this once and for all. I begged him to stay home, but he was determined."

"And what happened?"

She wilted. "He never came back. The next morning, I went to Perodin, who insisted he'd never seen my husband. This time I went to the police. They assured me they had spoken to Perodin and inspected the orchard but found nothing suspect. One policeman even suggested my husband was having an affair and would return when he was ready. Even if Hrolf didn't love me, he wouldn't have done that. He considers a man's principles more important than life itself. I fear his beliefs have resulted in his living death." She stared at me, her eyes pleading. "There is no one else to turn to. Mr. Frankenstein, you understand these things. You are a monster, no offense."

"None taken." It had been two years since I'd reinvented myself as a consulting detective, taking the name of my deceased creator. Though I still turned heads with my flat top and neck bolts, a significant portion of Geneva accepted me as an authority on monsters. "Clearly, something has detained your husband, but why do you think he's been turned into a zombie? It's 1821, after all."

"That's how Perodin gets people to work for him." She saw my disbelief and added, "If you heard those moans, you'd have no doubt. Please." She handed me a pencil drawing. "This is my husband."

I looked it over. Hrolf Kurzmann had a high forehead and bushy eyebrows, raised slightly. My attention was drawn by his eyes, deep and sad. That's where principles got you, though without them you became Perodin. I extended my hand, which engulfed hers. "I'll take the case."

The first step was to talk to Perodin. I'd heard the zombie rumors but attributed them to prejudice against foreigners. Even if the rumors were true, as a Swiss and a settled family man, Hrolf didn't fit the profile of the supposed victims. Still, as I stood outside the small one-story building that served as his store, something unnatural hung in the air that couldn't be blown away by Lake Geneva's blustery winds. Before going inside, I wandered along the ten-foot-high concrete wall that surrounded the property.

"Hey, you!" someone said with a heavy Creole accent. He was a squat, dark-skinned man with black, bristly hair and biceps that filled his sleeves. A thin mustache and a narrow tie gave him an aristocratic air.

"I was admiring the height of your wall," I said. "I'll bet you don't have a problem with apple theft. Are you the owner?"

"I am. You can find any kind of apples for sale inside my store."

"Actually, I wanted to talk to you."

His frown made it clear he didn't want to talk to me. "I sell apples, not conversation."

"I wasn't intending to pay for your words. Do you know Hrolf and Ada Kurzmann?"

He scratched his neck with long fingernails. "They own property abutting mine. Have they complained about me again? I can't help it if some of my workers sing at night. Many are far from home. I can't deny them the right to express themselves."

"Hrolf Kurzmann visited you Wednesday night and hasn't been seen since."

Perodin scowled. "Twice this man has complained about noise, but both times it was during the day. It doesn't make sense to come at night. I work hard and I'm a sound sleeper."

"I hear some of your workers keep busy at night, however."

"Some apple grinding is done then. This country's growing season is ridiculously short, so we can't waste any time." He glared at me. "Any time at all."

"Perhaps I could talk to some of your workers. I'm always trying to improve my Creole."

He bristled at my joke. "I can't help you."

I nodded. "In that case, I'll buy a bushel of apples."

Perodin reluctantly led me through his store. The interior reeked of his sweet, slightly spoiled product. Filled bags stood in rows on shelves that lined the wall. According to the signs, there were rubinettes, marigolds, and berner rosens. Attracted by their distinctive yellow, I bought a bag of arlets. It would take me a month to finish them, but I could offer them to clients.

I didn't leave with Hrolf Kurzmann, but I hadn't expected to. I needed to find out if the concrete wall was there to keep thieves out or workers and Kurzmann in. Night was the time to do that, and Igor was the man to help me.

•　　　•　　　•

Igor lived in a narrow, ramshackle house whose rent I subsidized to ensure he didn't end up in the street. While working for me, I could trust Igor with my life. Left to his own devices, however, his carousing often left him in such a state of depravity that it was hard to distinguish between his head and his hunchback.

As I opened his front door, a precariously placed flowerpot from the second-floor window glanced off the side of *my* head, the resulting lump ruining its flat symmetry. Miffed, I picked up a piece of the pot and discovered a telltale length of string attached to the door. I stalked into Igor's bedroom, the tossed wilds of his blankets offering glimpses of his head and right leg. My anger dissipated. He was the closest thing I had to a friend.

"Not much point in buying perennials if you're going to smash them after a couple of days," I said, holding the broken pot under his nose.

"That's my security system." He yawned. "It also doubles as a wake-up call."

"What if no one comes in?"

His head emerged from the blankets, his hair sticking straight as hay in all directions. "Then there's no point in getting up."

"Why don't you get the lock fixed?"

"Thieves keep breaking it. What do you want?"

I added "get Igor a better door and fix his lock" to my mental list. That would be easier than getting him out of jail if one of his flowerpots killed someone.

"Do you ever frequent Perodin Orchards?"

He grimaced. "I stay away from those apples."

I mentioned his usual fee, however, and he agreed to help me.

•　　•　　•

"If I come out of this with a belief in zombies, I'm holding you responsible," Igor said as we walked carefully along the wall. Shards of glass stuck out of the top like supplicating hands. The stars were out but no moon, offering just enough light to show we couldn't see much.

"We've encountered werewolves, vampires, and ourselves. Would meeting zombies make a difference to your worldview?" I asked, my body lurching forward as I stepped into a small hole.

"It might. I've pretty much freed myself of empathy, but even I might feel sorry for a zombie, unless he tried to eat me. Then all bets are off."

Igor liked to make himself sound harder than he was. In truth, he had been devoted to Victor Frankenstein. That devotion shifted to me after my creator's death, despite my indirect complicity in it.

I knelt and bid Igor to climb onto my shoulders. I then stood up and raised him to the top of the wall. "Mind the broken glass," I said. He swore, saying he minded it very much, then landed on the other side with an "oof!" I tossed over a rope, which he tied to a nearby tree trunk. I then pulled myself into the orchard.

Inside, each twisted tree looked like an angry old man standing his ground. I was struck by the silence. If Perodin had men working tonight, they were being quiet. For the most part, I preferred night, as it obscured my monstrous features and I felt almost normal. As Igor was a nocturnal tavern crawler, I figured he felt the same way. The darkness and silence inside Perodin's orchard gave us ample opportunity to imagine, however, and I found myself longing for the limitations of reality.

"Let's go," I said, pointing to a barn-like building I could make out in the distance. We walked, stray apples squishing under my feet. The barn was about two hundred feet long and a hundred feet wide. I pulled on its broad metal door but couldn't budge it. The building had randomly placed tiny, barred windows, like the eyes of a spider. We saw nothing through the grime. At least, I thought it was grime.

"This looks more like a prison than a place to store apples," I said.

"Or a torture chamber," Igor added.

We circled the barn but found no other entrance. I was about to suggest we make one, when the slow clump of heavy footsteps froze us in place. We watched a shadowy, bare-chested figure walk right past us. Once he was about thirty feet away, Igor exhaled heavily.

"You know why zombies never get anywhere in the world? They're not curious."

"Well, we are," I said, and we quietly followed him, maintaining a thirty-foot separation. Several times in the dark I stumbled over the uneven ground, once crashing to my knees, but it didn't matter. Our leader paid us no mind.

After about ten minutes the man vanished behind one of the taller trees. As we got closer, I kept expecting him to lurch into view, but he didn't. Igor circled the tree in question. In front of it, the ground sloped gently downward.

"How does a zombie vanish into thin air?" he asked.

I backed away from the tree, looked up at its branches, then in front of it. My eyes fell on a large pile of brush and limbs. "This doesn't look random." We dragged away the limbs and were hit by a belch of hot air. Beyond that was an iron-grated door and a tunnel. Peering inside we saw pinpoints of light and heard what sounded like the distant hum of machines and the banging of picks.

"I suppose you want to go down there," said Igor, without enthusiasm.

"I definitely don't want to go down there, but if Perodin really is using zombies, I have a feeling this is where they'd be."

Igor shook his head. "Me too."

The entrance opened into an eight-by-five foot tunnel and, fortunately for us, the ground was more dirt than rock. Using the walls as guides, we made our way down. About two hundred feet in we encountered our first flickering torch, mounted on the wall. It illuminated lines of wheel tracks.

After walking ten minutes, we saw in the distance a more concentrated light, beckoning like an ocean promising suffocation. The hum of machines, which had seemed so uniform, now sounded disjointed and random, a cacophony of grinding, hissing, and puffing, as well as ticking of pickaxes on rock.

Further down, the cavern opened onto an enormous room. The light of torches and several smelters danced, animating fifty stolid, plodding workers. Shadows, flickering light, and encroaching darkness twisted the images and grafted the impression of life onto the lifeless. Were they mining gold, silver, or diamonds? I couldn't tell, and they didn't seem to care.

"We can't overcome all of them," Igor whispered.

"We may not have to, if they really are zombies. They have their orders, but not the will to deviate from them. As long as we don't interfere, they should ignore us."

He looked at me with skepticism. "And what are we going

to do if we see Kurzmann? Say, *Congratulations on your new job. Nice colleagues?*"

"No, we're going to interfere."

We approached the horde. As predicted, the workers paid us no heed unless we bumped into one. This happened several times, with them so intent on their tasks and we unsure of our direction. I intentionally touched a few and sniffed their breath, but they were neither cold nor smelled of rot. Instead, they reeked of sweat. Some wore only rags, while others were absurdly overdressed as if for a night out that, without warning, turned into months of forced labor.

We shouted out Hrolf's name, but that got no reaction until one figure pushing a rock-laden barrow froze. I would not have recognized him. His hair was longer than in the picture, his body thinned and his sad eyes vacant.

"That is my name." His low, monotone voice seemed to scrape his vocal cords.

"We're here to rescue you," I said, motioning for Igor to come over to us.

Hrolf remained motionless. Did words have meaning to one with no will? That he knew his name showed he retained some memory. "Your wife is very worried."

His eyes flickered slightly, as if weighing an idea he couldn't quite grasp. His gaze drifted from my eyes to my body.

"I have no wife." He turned and resumed pushing his wheelbarrow.

Igor stared. "If that was Kurzmann, either he's changed or the man who drew his portrait is the worst artist ever."

"This place would change anybody."

"He was eating you with his eyes."

I wasn't sure. "He can look all he wants."

I picked up Hrolf and threw him over my shoulder. That got his attention, as well as everyone else's. He let out a strangled groan that shook me to the core, while the dead eyes of every other zombie turned toward us.

"Time to leave," I said to Igor. When I said "leave," my voice jumped an octave and stretched the syllable because Hrolf had bitten my arm. I dropped him with a punch, but instead of pursuing us, he rose to his feet and returned to his wheelbarrow. The others went back to their tasks. But when I took a few steps toward Hrolf, all dead eyes were on me again.

"Let the police handle this," said Igor. "They might even believe you."

I agreed, and we slowly retreated from the mine. Though backward glances didn't reveal anything, the clump of heavy footfalls was unmistakable.

"Do you think this is an escort?" Igor asked.

"Not to anywhere we want to go."

We increased our pace, but stumbling in the flickering darkness, we failed to shake our pursuers. I am not the fleetest of foot, but it would be embarrassing, or worse, to be outrun by zombies.

When we reached the opening of the mine and ripped away the branch cover, the wall of stars energized Igor, who left me in the dust. I found him cursing by the wall, unable to scale it by himself.

"They're right behind you!" he yelled, as I staggered up to him. In a single motion, I hoisted him to the top of the wall. As I looped the rope over it, I felt hands grabbing me. Soon I was surrounded by dead-eyed, expressionless faces. Fists rained down on me like anvils. I heard Igor screaming, though it might have been me.

●　　　●　　　●

I woke up on a table, like the one Victor Frankenstein had used when he'd brought me to life. Then, I'd been filled with curiosity. This time I was filled with the will of Edgard Perodin. He stood over me like one of his trees.

"You work for me now," he said. "Only Perodin Orchards matter. You will labor in my mine until you die."

I recalled a time when I was barely aware of Perodin, and another when it was important to stop him. I also remembered how I'd questioned my sense of worth and, as a creation of Victor Frankenstein, my right to be. All that was irrelevant now. The world made sense, and though I could not feel it, I knew the beauty of order and simplicity.

One of Perodin's laborers led me back into the mine. There was nothing to say as we walked through the flickering darkness. When I joined their cheerless ranks, the horde of workers offered no acknowledgement. I dug, smashed, hauled, and smelted, unquestioning as a machine. Only the growing ache in my muscles informed me of time's passing. I noticed Kurzmann occasionally and recalled I had been hired to save him. I also knew I would die in this mine. These and every other fact in my head were like trees in a picture I couldn't alter. At some point I was led out of the mine for another injection and a few hours' sleep.

Then I dug, smashed, hauled, and smelted.

Days passed like the wind.

At some point above the clatter and hum of work, I heard my name. I looked up to see Igor approaching me. Three staggering men flanked him.

"I went to the police," said Igor. "But either Perodin is paying them off or they don't listen to hunchbacks. I didn't know what to do, so I got drunk." He motioned to his colleagues, cowering from fear or drink. "Then I found these men to help. Another thing. The police were right about Kurzmann. He ran off with another woman. The Hrolf down here isn't our man."

I stared.

"And you can stop fantasizing about devouring me. That's not going to happen."

"I will not eat you," I said. "But you cannot obstruct my work."

"That's a problem because I cannot allow you to stay," said Igor.

He told his fellow carousers to grab onto me. Somewhere in my mind I recognized the humor of the scene, these fearful drunks contrasting with me and Perodin's work crew. There was no place for a laugh, however.

"Leave or die," I said.

Other workers circled my would-be rescuers. A Haitian placed a filthy hand on one of the drunks' shoulders. The drunk slapped it off. It was replaced by two others.

"You can't pay me enough to do this," the drunk stammered. He ran back up the tunnel, soon followed by the other two.

Igor looked at me and frowned. Even four men could not drag me out of the mine.

"I won't leave you down here!" he screamed, leaving me down there.

•   •   •

When I next woke up from the floor of the barn, Perodin stood over me.

"Igor is a problem. Kill him."

I felt clarity.

It was early morning as I walked three hours to Igor's house, one foot in front of the other. The streets of Geneva stirred with silent people, eyes down, on their way to work. Horse carts clattered, birds tweeted, smoke drifted from factory chimneys. Igor was difficult to locate at night, but most early mornings found him passed out in or near his bed. As I often visited him, no one would question my presence.

Igor was my friend and did not deserve to die, but the logic of killing him was unassailable. He would not give up. I had killed others—an innocent girl, Victor's fiancé, his friend, and indirectly, Victor himself—and in the past these actions had made me doubt the value of my existence. But today it was just information.

Yet as I stepped up to Igor's front door, something made me glance up, then turn the knob and brace for impact.

•   •   •

I was again on my back, this time in a hospital, my ankles hanging over the mattress. I felt woozy, but in the haze, I noticed something that had been missing: my will. Across from me was a disheveled Igor, snoring in a chair. I tossed my pillow at him.

"Ow!" he said, as he stood up and stretched, not that he was ever going to stand up straight. "I don't sleep well in chairs. Give me the floor any day."

"You give yourself to the floor just about every night. What happened?"

"You destroyed another of my plants. Did you forget it was there?"

"No." Yet something Perodin had not been able to control made me open that door. "What did the doctor say?"

"That you were pumped up with some drug. He wrote it down." Igor pulled a note from his pocket. "Tetrodotoxin. He also said you had traces of something else in you that might have diminished its effect slightly."

"Victor put all sorts of stuff into me."

"The doctor wrote the name of that down, too." He dug through every pocket he had, plus his waistband. "Must have lost it. Anyway, the tetrodotoxin is what made you obey Perodin. You need to stay here another twenty-four hours to get it all out of your system."

"What I need is to get Perodin." I swung my legs onto the floor. My gown caught on the frame, exposing my lack of clothes.

"Mother of God," Igor said, turning away.

•   •   •

After I got dressed, a horse cart whisked us to the police station. I showed them the injection holes in my arm and the doctor's report, and this time they listened. Three policemen accompanied us to Perodin's Orchard. A clerk summoned the owner to the store. When he saw me and Igor, his eyes widened, and he denied everything. He couldn't stop me from leading him and the police to his mine though. After we located the captive workers, Perodin sighed, then yelled, "Tear them ..." But before he could finish the sentence, I got him in a bear hug and placed my hand over his mouth. His workers, needing more complete instructions than that, continued their toil. Perodin's zombie exploitation had played out. As he was cuffed and led off the orchard, I couldn't resist a final question.

"Do you feel any remorse?"

He glowered. "About being caught?"

"No. About robbing men of their will and forcing them to do your bidding."

"I did my workers a favor," he said. "Hundreds of people labor in factories, bemoaning their lot. To what end? I gave them a goal, they achieved it, and felt a sense of accomplishment."

"You robbed them of what it means to be human," I said.

He laughed. "What does that mean?"

I was still working on that question, but I was more than willing to share my provisional answer.

"Having the right to hate people like you." I walked away.

It was a theatrical closing line, but as I thought about it later, it wasn't the existence of people like Perodin that most bothered me. Nor was it people like Kurzmann, supposedly a principled man who'd been able to rationalize abandoning his wife for someone else. Dealing with morally questionable people was my job. Because of my past, it was also my life. But Perodin had given me one more thing to question. I'd like to think a reserve of strength rather than diluted tetrodotoxin allowed me to choose getting crowned by Igor's flowerpot. Had that not happened, I would have done whatever nefarious deed the orchard owner had commanded. A frightening thought, but what unnerved me more was how much I enjoyed and missed the complete lack of conflict I had as a zombie.

5

None So Blind as Those Unseen

"C AN YOU DO ANYTHING FOR ME?" I asked. My plaintive tone must have sounded incongruous, coming from a seven-foot, flat-headed man. In contrast, Dr. Arensdorf was short and pudgy, with a forehead that reached to the top of his skull. As he studied my face, he seemed detached from the rest of the world.

"I normally deal in noses." His ad stated he'd spent a year in India, learning rhinoplasty techniques. A mounted map of the country, a jeweled statue of an elephant, a stuffed cobra, snake, and a painting of the Taj Mahal adorned his cluttered office.

I often wondered how my life might have been different had Victor given me a more pleasing appearance. I could have married, raised a family, and not killed my creator. But I always arrived at the same answer: I am what I am and tried not to dwell on what I couldn't change. But the newspaper ad caught my attention.

"Do you use those?" he asked, pointing to the bolts protruding from both sides of my neck.

"Not since I was animated," I said. "I'm reluctant to remove them, however, in case I ever need another jolt."

He scratched his cleft chin. "I can soften the flatness of your head and cover some scars." As I hesitated, he added, "You would be closer to normal."

That was what I wanted yet hearing him say "closer to normal" reminded me of what I'd never be.

"I'll think about it," I said.

As I left, he pressed an ornately lettered card into my hand.

•   •   •

Back in my office, I glanced through the newspaper to confirm the publication of my own advertisement for detective services. I found it on page 3, surrounded by ads for knives, stoves, and nails, and a couple of articles. One cursed the problem of thieving gypsies. The other related how two mansions in the city had been burnt down under suspicious circumstances. Perhaps I could find work looking into that. Then again, fires were not uncommon in Geneva, and they weren't my favorite thing.

The wind shrieked outside, its fist smashing against my windows. My door swung open, and in its wake stood a sad-eyed man with curly dark hair and a short mustache. He wore a ruby red vest over a white-collared shirt. His teeth were clenched, as if to prevent the escape of heat. He looked me over.

"You must be Frankenstein."

"I must be."

"My name is Conrad Hausler. I own a successful jewelry business." He paused when I didn't respond. "The problem is my daughter, Adele, who has disappeared." He showed me a drawing of an attractive, young woman with long dark hair and a haughty expression, wearing a clinging dress.

I nodded. "I could help you find her."

He frowned. "I don't need help with that. She's at home."

Sometimes Geneva's extreme weather left even its wealthier residents addled. "I don't understand."

"Due to an accident, she's become literally invisible."

I folded my arms. "In that case, you'd better start at the beginning."

He winced, as if the beginning was the worst part.

"Adele is seventeen years old," said Hausler, "and quite striking, at least she was when you could still see her. She attracted plenty of attention and had her pick of normal, promising lads. Instead, she picked Griffin, who is insane."

"How does he manifest his handicap?"

"I knew from the start that he was trouble. First, he's fifteen years older. Second, he has crazy ideas about how everyone—the richest man to the poorest homeless person—should be equal. Third, he's a scientist. I think he saw my daughter as an experiment."

"You said she became invisible."

"After about a month, Griffin didn't want to see her anymore. I said, *Good. We finally agree on something.* But that just made Adele more determined. She kept finding pretexts to meet him, until finally, he lost his temper and tossed a vial of his invisibility solution at her."

"This is something he developed?"

"Yes."

I'd heard theories of a solution that refracted light, rendering invisibility, but I'd never given them much credence. "Do you know where he lives?"

Hausler shook his head. "He fled shortly after dousing my daughter. She says the effect is temporary, but it's been a week, and she is still completely invisible."

"Do you know if he ever doused himself?"

"Regularly. He uses invisibility to practice his main source of income, which is theft."

"Mr. Hausler, I'm not sure what you want me to do. Geneva has scientists that could possibly help your daughter."

"This man has damaged her reputation. He'd like to turn Swiss society upside-down. He's a threat to the upper class. I want him brought to justice."

I doubted there was a law against turning people invisible, and I knew there wasn't one against men compromising women's honor. Griffin's capture wouldn't restore Adele's name.

"How is he a threat to the upper class?"

"Adele has repeated his rants against us, that we should surrender our wealth to the poor, after all the work I've done to get ahead. Can you imagine the havoc an invisible man could impart on the wealthy?"

"But as far as you know, he's done nothing except talk about it."

"I told you, he is a thief."

"I can try to find him, but it seems the only crime he's committed against you directly is make your daughter invisible. If your daughter reappears in the meantime, I don't see what he can be prosecuted for, unless he's caught in the act of stealing."

He leveled a glare at me. "I'm the one who wants to hire you. Are you interested or not?"

If Adele did not reappear, then this Griffin should be held responsible. I thought of the many times I wished I were invisible, but I couldn't imagine it as a permanent condition. And Adele was at an age where, above all, she would want to be seen.

"I will take the case."

"Thank you. Here's a drawing of Griffin."

It was actually a drawing of his clothes, which completely covered him. These included a black bowler hat, facial bandages, dark glasses, a long overcoat, and white gloves. He looked like a bit of a dandy, and I thought, here is the one time where clothes definitely made the man.

"How did you get this?" I asked.

"Adele has artistic talent. She drew both pictures."

"Tell me more about her."

"She's my youngest. I have two older sons that work in my business. They are married and live in the city. I never worry about them, but Adele has given me nothing but consternation. She's impulsive and thinks that life is about doing what you want. Unless you discredit Griffin, I don't know how she'll ever marry."

"Did you have some prospects in mind?"

"We've tried to set her up with several responsible, pious, hardworking men, but Adele automatically rejects anyone we suggest."

"And chooses mad scientists instead."

Hausler scratched his bushy eyebrow, leaving its hairs sticking outward.

"I believe she bases her choices solely on what would most disappoint us."

I doubted that, but that was probably a fringe benefit. After Hausler accepted my fee, I asked to meet Adele.

•   •   •

Faded pink curtains lined the one window in Adele's bedroom. The wallpaper was sea green with small swirls of white. An oak dresser, a large beech framed armchair, a dressing table and mirror, and a bookcase filled the room. On the shelves, in front of the books, which appeared to be mostly fairy tales and fantasies, perched six wide-eyed dolls. Adele sat sprawled on the armchair, though I could see only her white puffy skirt, a black top, and black boots. It was like looking at a clothes advertisement without a model. Her parents stood by the open door.

"Adele, what is your opinion of Jack Griffin?" I asked.

"I hate him." Her voice, for a girl, was low and almost masculine sounding.

"Your father wants me to find him. Do you?"

"I don't care what you do."

From the anger in her voice, I guessed that she did. "You believe your invisible condition is temporary?" I asked.

"Jack had to re-inject and douse himself every so often to maintain the effect."

"Both?"

"Dousing covers the outside. If you don't inject, the organs are visible."

"So, Griffin did both to you?"

"Yes."

I could picture him dousing someone in anger but injecting her as well made the action seem more calculated.

"Do you have any idea what was in the solution?"

"That's not the kind of thing we shared," she said coolly.

"Did he have any plans for his invisibility solution?"

She went silent for a moment. "He believes people are limited by their appearance. Invisibility liberates what's inside. But all I know of his plans is they don't include me."

"Has he any friends, besides you?"

"Not that I know of. He spent most days working in his rooms, but he often went out at night."

I tried to question Adele's mother, but she deferred to her husband in all matters. Hausler gave me Griffin's former address. Later, I would talk to the landlady. First, I needed to pay a visit to Igor.

•   •   •

I found him at home, lying in his customary position, in his bed, flat on his stomach. Because of his hunchback, he couldn't lay supine. He greeted me with his customary civility.

"Get out of here," he muttered, pulling his rumpled blankets over his head.

"If you don't want visitors, maybe you should lock your door."

"And worry about losing my key? I couldn't take the tension. What do you want?"

"I need your help. We have to find an invisible man."

"Haven't seen him," he deadpanned. "Though if I drink enough, I could see multiples of him at the same time."

I explained that that was, in effect, the direction I wanted him to go. If Jack Griffin went out a lot and tried to spread his philosophy on invisibility, his most willing listeners might be found at some of the same disreputable taverns Igor frequented.

"This man could be dangerous, so don't drink too much," I said.

"Don't worry," Igor said, gingerly lowering his legs to the floor. "I know my limit. I ought to. I've gone over it enough times."

I next visited Griffin's last address. The house was nestled on a quiet street, overlooking Lake Geneva. It surprised me that a scientist would choose to live in such a visually distracting place.

Madame Leveque was a widow who rented out five of her rooms. She was a short, earnest-looking woman, about sixty years old. She insisted on making me some tea before she'd answer my questions. We sat in her kitchen.

"We get all kinds here, of course," she said, sipping from her steaming cup. "But I had little idea what *all* meant until I met Jack Griffin."

"Have you any idea where he went?"

"No, and I'd like to. He owes me for three weeks."

"What was he like?"

"I cook for my lodgers and generally we eat together. I like to get to know who I live with, even if it's temporary. Especially if it's temporary. But Griffin made no attempt to know anyone. He insisted I bring his meals to his room. He kept the door locked. At first, I thought he was shy because he was a foreigner. He didn't speak French very well and had a thick English accent. Later, I learned he didn't care what anyone thought of him."

"Did he ever go out?"

"Rarely during the day. He often went out at night, however, and returned very late. A few times he brought a woman with him. I can just imagine what kind of woman it was, and I told him I didn't allow that sort of thing under my roof. He always apologized, but that had no effect on his behavior. My late husband Basil would have thrown him out, but I'm just an old lady and, well, I need the income."

"I'm curious about these women. Do you think they were different or the same one?"

She cupped her chin. "Now that you mention it, I think it was mainly one woman the last few weeks he was here. Several times they made a terrible racket, throwing things, raised voices, especially hers. This is a well-built house, but it doesn't take much to wake everyone up in the middle of the night."

"Did you hear anything that was said?" I asked.

"Well, I didn't want to hear anything in the wee hours, and her language was coarse, unlike Griffin's, who despite his lack of personality, could turn on the charm when necessary. I think she said something like, *You can't discard me like a torn glove*, and *Don't your words mean anything?*"

"Not the type of thing a prostitute would say."

She shuddered. "I suppose not."

This supported Hausler's story that Griffin had tired of Adele. I asked if he'd left anything behind. She led me to a pantry. In a corner were three notebooks, some beakers, and a syringe. I leafed through the books, but they were written in a code of symbols that meant nothing to me. I pocketed the syringe, figuring it might possess a secret, then bid Madame Leveque good-bye and told her I'd be in touch about her lost rent if I located Griffin.

Despite my connection to Victor, my scientific knowledge was limited to that of a well-read layman. I knew a man who worked at the city hospital, however, and asked him to check the syringe.

The next morning a messenger delivered a note from Igor to my office. In scrawled, uneven letters, it said, "Griffin frequents the Le Perroquet Noir." I wrote a message for Igor to meet me there that night at 8 p.m.

•   •   •

For most things, Igor was late, but he was punctual on the job. The exception was when we were supposed to meet in a pub. Then he was early. I found him in a booth, chatting up a buxom waitress.

"This is the man I work for," Igor explained to the waitress as I sat down opposite him. "He may be tall, but he's also ugly. As a matter of fact ... what did you say your name was?"

"Waitress," she said, her expression fixed in a way that encouraged conciseness.

"Mine's Igor," my partner said. "I tell you that just so you'll know whose name to shout in case we're ever intimate."

"Would you like to order something?" Waitress asked. "Other than a drink thrown in your face? That's part of our service for people like you."

"We'll have two draughts of lager, if you please," I interjected. As she left, I glared at Igor. "Try to keep your questionable charms hidden. We need cooperation, not altercations."

"I'm just letting her know that there's two sides to hunchbacks."

"And ironically, she'd prefer to see the back of you."

"Funny," he said, finishing his mug of beer.

Le Perroquet Noir was doing good business for early on a weeknight. Out of about forty seats, only two tables and a booth were empty, along with some stools at the bar. While none of the customers looked as odd as us, even in the dimmed light, everyone looked a bit off. I could easily imagine what imperfections makeup and lowered hats covered.

"Is there anyone here we should talk to?" I asked Igor.

The waitress set our tankards in front of us. Igor took a deep gulp, brushing the foam off his mouth. "As a matter of fact ..." He nodded toward the bartender, a hulking man disfigured with tattoos, a billy-goat beard, and a closed left eye. "They call him Cyclops. Can't imagine why. Maybe he lives in a cave with sheep. He denied knowing Griffin, but the waitress said Cyclops and Griffin were like best friends. I got nothing out of him, but maybe between the two of us ..."

"He doesn't look subtle. Let's try a direct approach," I said.

We slid onto two stools in front of the beer tap. Cyclops stopped wiping the bar and gave us a dirty look. He might have lacked depth perception, but he clearly conveyed we were closer than he liked.

"We're looking for a man with a bandaged head, scarf, and dark glasses," I said.

His eye met ours, holding its own despite being outnumbered. "Yeah?"

"We hear he's in here a lot, that you two are ... thick as thieves."

"Shove off," he growled. "Take humpback with you."

Igor shook off slights from friends but never forgot them when uttered by enemies, and I was his only friend. He leaned forward, his back arching higher than his head. "You have an *eye* for rude comments."

I reached for Cyclops's shoulder to reassure him, but he pulled back. "We heard he's figured out a way to become invisible," I said. "Our appearances have given us nothing but grief. To the man that could free us from our humiliation, we would swear undying allegiance. We'll be here for a few hours."

My speech ended. Cyclops's was over minutes ago when he said, "Shove off." I told Igor we should get back to our drinks before flies fell into them.

I nursed my lager, while Igor put away two or three. He became even ruder in front of the waitress, who after an hour probably made a mortal enemy by switching with another girl. I knew, however, Igor would reassert himself into a no-nonsense mode if need be. That need occurred fifteen minutes before closing time, when the invisible man slid next to Igor.

"You have been talking about me," he said. His head, as advertised, was completely bandaged up. He wore the black bowler hat, dark glasses, and white gloves. An overcoat and turned-up collar completed his outfit.

"We're interested in your invisibility solution," I said.

He looked me over. "I can see why."

"I hear you developed a philosophy about it. Tell us about it. A brilliant scientist such as yourself should be known."

Griffin rubbed his covered chin. I wondered if itching was an issue. "It's no secret. If you possess good looks, you feel compelled to maintain them. If you are ugly, you are defensive and dismissive of those that aren't. In either case, the real you, inside, is diverted. My invisibility drug liberates you."

I glanced at Igor, who stared at his drink, pretending not to listen. Griffin continued.

"You two are perfect examples. People see you and recoil. You feel that you have to adapt to society's norms. Instead of being *you*, and developing your strengths, you become *them*. It's a kind of suicide."

"Isn't becoming invisible like donning a mask?" I asked.

"On the contrary. People would then be able to see beyond appearances and listen to other people's ideas. Wouldn't you prefer that people see you that way, instead of reacting in fear or hate?"

"Of course." I wasn't ready to share that I'd visited a surgeon the day before in hopes of achieving that very goal. "How does this serum work? How long do its effects last?"

"That depends on the dose and the person. The dose I use lasts 72 hours." He stared at Igor. "You don't talk much."

"He doesn't waste words, at least not to men. How can we gain your trust?" I asked.

Before he could answer, Igor scratched his back, and a red-faced man whose nose appeared to have met multiple fists loomed over us. He was shaped like a chest of drawers.

"What happened to you, friend?" he said to Griffin, each word as thick as his body. "It must cost you a fortune in bandages. Did you lay with a porcupine or something, or are you just protecting us from the ugliest man alive?"

Griffin and I sat stunned. Compared to us, Griffin looked like a theater star. The only person who responded was Igor, who clasped on the man's right arm and said, "He is not your friend."

The red-faced man squealed as Igor increased pressure, then wrestled him to the ground and kicked him several times, until he lay still. Cyclops picked up what was left and tossed it out of the tavern. Griffin stared again at Igor. Invisible, he possessed the ultimate poker face, but through the bandages he emitted an air of appreciation.

"I like your style," he said.

"It's not a style," said Igor.

We sat silent for about fifteen seconds, except for Igor, who was breathing heavily.

"I want to change society for the better, but I can't do it by myself," Griffin said finally. "If you're serious, meet me here at noon on Thursday. We'll talk more." He stood up and walked out.

"Should we follow him?" Igor asked.

Neither of us were nimble tracers, nor did I want to jeopardize our invitation. "We've met him. Let's see what Thursday brings." I looked him in the eye. "Who was the man you beat up?"

He smiled. "A drinking associate. You owe him some money."

•   •   •

Tuesday morning when I walked into my office, I had a feeling someone besides me had been in it. On top of the clutter on my desk lay a paper from the Perodin case, which I'd closed a month ago. Had I noticed it before, I would have returned it to its proper folder. I went to my cabinet and checked the Griffin folder. Everything seemed in order. Dealing with an invisible man was enough to make anyone suspicious, but I resolved to take nothing for granted.

Wednesday morning, I received two messages, one from my doctor friend and the other from Hausler. The doctor had analyzed Griffin's discarded syringe and found traces of Monocane, an addictive drug that steeped its users into paranoia and monomania. I sent out another message, asking how dangerous one dose would be.

The second message was from Hausler: Adele had reappeared. I walked back to their house. On the way, only three streets from my office, I passed the twisted hulk of another burned-out house. I did hate fire.

Father and daughter sat at the dining room table as Frau Hausler led me in. They had been arguing when I entered the house but stopped when they saw me. Adele looked pale, her long dark hair worn with bangs over her eyes. When she brushed the bangs aside, those eyes flashed anger at her father. She wore loose, dull-colored clothing. I told them I'd seen Griffin, or at least his occupied clothes, at the Le Perroquet Noir the night before. I didn't know where he lived, but I expected to learn more soon.

"Now that the effects of the solution have worn off, do you still want me to pursue this?" I asked.

"I do," Hausler said. "My daughter's visibility doesn't change what he did to her. I'm going on a business trip in a day or two, but I will return as soon as I can."

At that moment, Adele stood up. "I'm going for a walk."

"You need to rest and allow that poison to fully pass through your system."

"I'll rest outside," said Adele. As she turned to go, her father grabbed her arm. Both glared, then Hausler pulled her into her room, locking her in. He pocketed the key and gave me a rueful look.

"She's been uncontrollable since she met that devil Griffin. I had to keep her locked up while she was invisible or God knows what she would have done."

"With your permission, I'd like to talk to her one more time, alone."

His cheek reddened. "She doesn't talk when she's like this."

I insisted, however, and he let me in. Adele had thrown herself face-down onto her bed.

"Where did you get those needle marks on your arm?" I hadn't seen any, but I figured I'd call her bluff. When she said nothing, I added, "Maybe I'll mention to your father that you took the invisibility drug numerous times, that it was your idea."

She turned to me. "What do you want?"

"Why did you take it?"

"Because I wanted to. My father thinks I fall in love every week, but he doesn't understand anything. I have latched onto some men, but only because I want to get out of here. Griffin was different though. He really believed in equality, and he was doing something about it."

"So why did you separate?"

"He thinks I'm a spoiled rich girl. I told him that was his own prejudice, which just made him angry. I was ready to give up my class privileges for real freedom. Though I don't like needles, I started taking his drug. At first, he was supportive, but Monocane made him arrogant and suspicious. He said invisibility didn't change what I was."

"If you took the drug multiple times, you must have been staying with Griffin."

"I was."

Whatever Griffin's long-range goals were, at best he probably realized that an emotional attachment to a 17-year-old woman left him vulnerable. At worst, he'd simply taken what he could.

"I know this is hard to accept," I said, "but he used you. He got you addicted, had his fun, and then moved on. You need to do the same."

She didn't answer.

•   •   •

Thursday at noon Igor and I returned to the Le Perroquet Noir. The tavern was half empty. I had a feeling someone who wanted to change the world wouldn't be a clock-watcher, and I was right. I ordered a bowl of porridge and a half loaf of bread while Igor gnawed on a half chicken. The waitress was a thick, hard-faced woman who gave the impression she didn't like them big and ugly, so I cautioned Igor to go easy on the small talk. Instead of Cyclops, a husky, gray-bearded man we'd never seen before tended the bar.

An hour passed. I sipped my porridge as it went from piping hot to pitifully brisk. We were about to leave when both Griffin and Cyclops entered.

"I apologize for my lateness," said Griffin. "But patience is a virtue when it comes to change."

"So, what are we doing?" I asked.

"Conducting an experiment. Follow me."

Griffin led us outside the tavern to an enormous fir tree. From his pocket he pulled out a syringe. "Sympathy for a cause is one thing. Action is another. To truly see what is inside a person, you must first be liberated by invisibility."

I stared at the syringe. In his second message the doctor who'd analyzed the solution assured me that one dose was safe, as long as there was never a second. Then again, I had no way of knowing if this was the same solution. Griffin noticed my concern.

"No one likes needles because all they see is the sharp point. I assure you; the invisibility solution is perfectly safe. I am the proof." He sunk the syringe into a bottle of dark liquid. "Additional proof is Adele Hausler." Of course, he knew I was working for her father.

"What about your friend?" I motioned toward Cyclops.

"Monsieur Allard? asked Griffin. "As it happens, he is more valuable to me visible." Cyclops said nothing, while Griffin beamed at Igor and me. "Who's first?"

"How long will it last?" asked Igor.

"No more than a couple of days. You won't notice any difference until I douse you, however."

"When will that be?" I asked.

"Tomorrow, if all goes well. It takes that long for the injection to take effect."

I exposed my left arm. "Go ahead." He told me to make a fist, then jammed me with the needle. Other than a prick and a slight metallic taste, I didn't feel anything. He then injected Igor.

"Now what?" I asked.

"Return here tomorrow at nine p.m. I'll douse you, the effect of which is immediate, and then, we'll give you a task."

"When you say nine p.m., do you mean nine or ten?" Igor asked.

"Nine," said Griffin.

Later, Igor and I discussed what we were getting into. As Griffin had said, after we left, we noticed no effects from the injection. Hausler had mentioned that the invisibility solution had changed his daughter's personality, though that could just have been her rebelliousness. Adele also said that Griffin had become increasingly arrogant, however, and he had been taking the solution the longest.

We wondered what the task would be. Griffin didn't like privileged people, so I suspected he might want us to rob a bank or something. I decided only I would show up for our appointment. Igor would arrive earlier and follow from a distance.

I didn't have to wait the next evening. Cyclops was behind the bar with the grey-bearded man we'd seen the day before.

"Where's humpback?" he asked as I approached.

"He doesn't like waiting."

"Neither do I. Come with me," he said, leading me upstairs to what I guessed were his living quarters. His three rooms were small and unassuming. It struck me that all of us, Griffin, myself, Igor, and Cyclops had no family. Cyclops lit a lantern that provided just enough light so I could see the lack of cheer in his rooms. He pointed to the water closet. "You can't see it, but in there is a tub filled with the invisibility solution. You're going to take your clothes off, get in, and make sure it covers all of you, including your eyes. We'll wait fifteen minutes for it to dry, then you can put your clothes back on."

I disrobed and got in the tub. The lower half of my body vanished instantly. After I finished submerging myself, I had difficulty getting out, as if my eyes were closed. My right foot accidentally kicked the tub, spilling the solution on the floor and making a spot vanish. Fortunately, the other side of the floorboard remained dry so the customers in the dining room below couldn't see what we were doing.

After the fifteen minutes passed, I got dressed. Cyclops provided white gloves, glasses, and a hat, all a bit tight. He also wrapped white bandages around my face. I still felt worthy of stares, but in an anonymous way, as if I were in costume.

"Where's Griffin?" I asked, as we walked down the stairs.

"I'm handling things today," said Cyclops. He said to wait outside for a moment. He returned with a small sack flung over his back. "Let's go."

We walked into a familiar part of town. The city was largely sleeping. The few pedestrians we encountered looked away and said nothing. I couldn't see Igor, but I assumed he was close by. After a forty-minute walk, we stopped in front of Conrad Hausler's home.

"Gather up some kindling," said Cyclops. A wooded area ringed around the back of the house.

"We're burning down this house?" I asked. I should have figured it out. Griffin had been the one burning down Geneva's mansions.

"Do you have a problem with that?"

"I'm having trouble reconciling Griffin's vision of equality with arson," I said.

"You don't need to. He's the thinker. You're the doer."

I liked to think of myself as both. I looked around and spotted Igor partially hidden behind a tree, about forty feet away. As I hesitated, Cyclops pulled out a revolver from his bag.

"You fire that and it will wake up everyone in the house," I said.

"That won't matter to you."

"What's your stake in this? I can see how you might want to be invisible, but Griffin doesn't allow it. Plus, you own your own pub, which gives you more in common with Hausler than the exploited poor."

Cyclops slapped me with his left hand. "What did I say? You are a doer, or you're done."

I rubbed my face. I thought I tasted blood but as I was invisible, I couldn't see it. Cyclops might be a loose plank in Griffin's plans, but I couldn't pry him away yet. "Kindling," I said, and I slowly walked to the back of the house. As I gathered some twigs, Cyclops keeping guard, I angled myself toward Igor. He could get the pistol from Cyclops. We could then bring him to the authorities and, with some pressure, get him to implicate Griffin in the fires. I walked to within ten feet in front of Igor, bracing for his attack, but it didn't happen. What was he waiting for? I guessed the answer a second before I suffered my second punch to the face and fell to my knees.

"Trust is important to me," Griffin's familiar voice said. A floating revolver pointed at my face. Cyclops leveled his gun at Igor.

"My head is important to me," I said.

"Then you should take measures not to lose it. I have singular ways to check on obedience."

I asked Igor if he was okay. He said he was fine, except not even for double wages would he spend twenty minutes hiding behind a tree with a naked man again. They had us gather armfuls of kindling and place it by Hausler's front door.

"Now what?" I asked Griffin.

"This house will be burned down. The only variable was whether you and your friend watched from inside or out. Sadly, you've opted for the former."

"How are you going to get us inside without waking the family?" I asked.

A skull-sized rock rose, hovered in front of a window, then smashed through.

"The family is not at home."

Hausler had told me he was going on a business trip. I hadn't realized he was taking the family. That seemed odd. And how did Griffin know? Were he and Adele still communicating?

Cyclops picked up another rock and cleared out enough space for him to crawl through the window. In a minute he had the front door unlocked. Griffin ushered Igor and me inside, using his pistol as a prod. From his bag, Cyclops got a chain and secured Igor to the staircase railing. With another chain he fastened me to a ceiling beam. He then grabbed an armful of kindling and walked upstairs.

"The thing is," said Griffin, "monocane, like any drug, can be tolerated only up to a point. For you two I am going to administer ten times the normal dose. By the time anyone is able to see your bodies, they will be bare bones. Somewhat charred, of course."

An imposing-looking syringe rose into the air. I braced against my bonds but couldn't loosen them.

"Your utopia seems a bit one-sided," I said.

Griffin laughed cruelly. "I'm not interested in being understood by the likes of you. There's a world of people out there who are never listened to. With this, I avenge the invisible, the unseen, the ignored."

I'd wanted to join that group, but I was not feeling avenged. Griffin proved invisibility came with a price.

"My creator was like you," I said. "He also had great gifts but misused them. He forgot he was a human being and thought he was God. Arrogance makes you invisible to yourself. When that happens, you become ... morally untethered."

"While you are physically tethered," said Griffin, pointing his syringe at my bound arms. If I was going down, I'd do it with a glare. It unfroze when I smelled smoke. Cyclops was nowhere to be seen. He had made his move and left. I lunged and grasped onto Griffin's wrist with my right hand. He struggled, kicking at me, but I held fast.

"At least you don't have to worry about the animals feasting on your decaying remains," I said to Griffin.

"Let go, you fool!" he screamed. "I have the key to your chains. If you let me go, I will free you."

"Could you put that in writing? You can use your invisible ink."

But without clothes, there was no place he could have carried the keys. I felt him twist in what had to be a painful position. With the room filling with smoke, I could just make out his figure. "If you don't let me go, we'll all die," he gasped.

"That's the idea," I said, though I was about ready to scream myself. A ball of flame shot through the open door and caught on the carpet where Griffin and I stood. I felt Griffin go limp, and I let him drop to the floor. Above me, the ceiling crackled. Perhaps, for once, fire and I could be on the same side. I said to Igor, "I'm going to see if I can upend this beam, but it may bring the house down."

He was kicking the railing, to no avail. "If it does, at least you don't have to worry about your head getting any flatter."

I pulled against the beam, but it barely budged. Lack of oxygen made me feel faint. I must have loosened something though, because a piece of the wooden ceiling did come down, on top of Griffin. I called out his name, but he didn't answer. I braced for one more tug that might squash us all. I lunged, heard a crack, and fell to the floor. Dazed, I pulled off my chain and staggered upright. With my oversized right foot, I smashed the smoldering railing and freed Igor. We dragged each other out of the burning building. Outside, all we could do was gasp and watch.

●　　　●　　　●

Hausler returned a week later, without his wife or Adele. I met him at his jewelry shop, where he temporarily lodged while he looked for another place to live. He stood behind an encased exhibit of watches, tapping the glass. I thought his curly hair had acquired some gray in our absence.

"How is your family?" I asked.

"My wife is shaken up. She keeps saying if we'd been home, this might not have happened. I say we might all be dead. The house was insured."

"It is fortunate you took them both on your business trip. Do you often do that?"

He hesitated. "No."

"How is Adele?"

"At some point she will see her encounter with that scoundrel for the tragedy it is. For now, she will live with a relative, away from here. She needs a new start."

She did, but if my guess was right, she wouldn't get one. When I saw the picture of Adele, she wore a daring, form-fitting dress. When she reappeared, she wore loose vestments. Then her father sent her away with a relative, but the business trip was a pretext. It was Griffin's baby she was going to have, a fact Hausler learned once her invisibility wore off.

"I believe Griffin died in the fire," I said. "As you know, his body was never found, but animals could have disposed of him. If he escaped, I believe the invisibility solution will eventually render him completely insane, and he will turn up."

"Adele told me his plan, to liberate everyone's inner self from their outer self." He threw up his hands. "Crazy."

"I agree. We are what we are. One of his partners, the owner of the Le Perroquet Noir, was arrested and questioned. He insists Griffin died. Regardless, I don't think he'll bother your daughter again." Except Griffin's name would now be forever associated with Adele and her child. "If you'd like to wait a few months on the second half of my fee ..."

"No," he said. "No ill will intended, but I would like to end our association."

A week later, after receiving a reminder in the post, I came to the same conclusion about my association with Dr. Arensdorf, the surgeon who had promised to change my appearance. Calling on my new ally, I lit a match, held it to Arensdorf's impressive card, and dropped it into the fireplace.

6

What Lies Beneath the Bandages

I GOR AND I WERE WALKING OFF a late dinner I'd treated him to, in celebration of solving the Invisible Man case. A light rain began to fall when we'd reached Geneva's most notorious waterfront street. In the dark, it looked deserted, but I knew prostitutes, thieves, and vagrants lurked among the old, misshapen buildings. At seven feet tall, with a flat head and hulking shoulders, no one ever accosted me more than once, while Igor was more at home here than the room I subsidized for him. Yet we both hesitated when a scream shattered the silence. Thinking someone needed help, we ran toward the cry and saw a young woman slapping away the bandaged hands of a mummy.

"Hey!" I yelled. The mummy turned stiffly in our direction, shook its right fist, then fled. Igor and I pursued the assailant for about 100 feet, but for a mummy he was fast, and we weren't. As we clumped back to the woman's side, she saw Igor's hunchback and my protruding electrodes and screamed a second time.

"I assure you, we pose no threat," I said, backing off. "My name is Frankenstein. I'm a detective, and this is my assistant Igor. Are you all right?"

She looked us over, something that rarely did us credit.

"I think so." She was short, wearing a hood and overcoat. While it wasn't expensive, it looked warm and fashionable, not the type of thing worn by the lower classes. Her eyes flashed anger instead of fear.

"Why were you being attacked ... by a mummy?" I asked.

"You're really detectives?"

"I swear on my creator's laboratory," I said.

Her eyes widened, but perhaps because of my earnest look, she then relaxed. "His name is Het Omari. He works in the Egyptian room of the Musee Histoire."

"As an exhibit?" asked Igor.

"No, he's in charge. I am his assistant."

"Are you sure it was him?" I asked. The man was completely covered in bandages.

"Yes. He wears a distinctive cologne that I noticed immediately."

Igor nodded. "I imagine odor is a concern for mummies."

She glared, not sure what to make of him. I knew what to make of Igor, but I couldn't make him be polite. "We'd like to help," I said, "but I still don't understand why you were attacked. Or why you are out here alone this time of night."

She appeared near tears. "My husband—you may have heard of Thomas Chastain?" Our blank faces revealed our ignorance. "In certain circles he's an acclaimed Romantic poet. Unfortunately, those circles aren't lucrative, so I work at the museum to defray expenses. It was a satisfactory arrangement until Omari started objecting to my husband's poetry."

"He's an expert on poetry, too?" I asked.

"His objection is not with the quality but the subject matter. Many of my husband's poems extol my beauty."

Though her hood obscured the top of her head, even a monster such as I could tell this woman possessed a natural attractiveness, unlike the painted faces one normally saw on this corner. "He disagrees?" I asked.

"He doesn't believe a husband should publish intimate details about his wife. It's as if he's from another time."

"Do you need someone to bring him up to 1821?" I asked.

Her eyes widened. "No! Please, I can't lose this job."

"So, your husband lets you work and walk alone at night?" asked Igor.

"He is ill. The one thing that helps is a certain medication available only from unorthodox sources."

I wondered if her husband had a drug dependency. If so, that problem would rival being attacked by mummies.

"Can we walk you home, then?" I offered. "Mummies aren't the only dangerous things loose at night."

"All right." She lived a mile out of our way, but I had wanted to walk. We learned her name, Renee, but not much else. We dropped her off at a small, rundown cottage. I gave her my calling card and wished her well. She thanked us and vanished inside, though her features stayed in my mind. I turned to Igor.

"What do you make of that?"

"Her or the mummy?"

"The mummy. I can guess what you think of her."

"I try to avoid men who dress up as mummies. They're either crazy or dead. Also, if I was going to accost someone, I'd do it in something less conspicuous, like an Easter Rabbit outfit."

"Wearing telltale cologne is equally foolish. It could be a setup."

That night I found myself sympathizing with Renee. It was a harsh world and she seemed alone, yet defiant. I had a feeling, and perhaps a hope, that we'd hear from her again. Instead, within two days I received a note telling me to stay away from her. It wasn't signed, but as the only person who saw me with Renee was the mummy, I figured I'd better pay Het Amari a visit.

• • •

I'd never been to the Musee Histoire. It's not that I wasn't interested in history. I just figured it would be hard to lose myself in its exhibits while everyone was staring at me. As I walked by its imitation Greek columns, however, I imagined a distant time of Plato and Aristotle discussing philosophical issues. It seemed appealing, until I remembered Greeks worshipped the human body. I made Hephaestus look like Adonis.

An attendant told me Omari's office was in the east wing of the building, just after the ancient Egyptian room. As I passed an administrative office, I saw a middle-aged man wearing a bright red cravat with his broad arms around Renee. She had her back to me and was leaning on him. *This woman believes in unorthodox work relationships*, I thought, and kept walking so she wouldn't see me.

Omari's office door was ajar as I walked by papyruses, statues, and a full-size mummy. A short man with close-cropped hair and a thin mustache smoked a cigarette and read a book at his desk

"That mummy looks healthy for its age," I said, sticking my head through the doorway.

"It's younger than you or me. I made it," he said, eyes glued to his book. When he looked up, he did a double take, but only one. "What can I do for ... you?"

"You don't know who I am?"

"I'd remember you."

I handed him the note. "You didn't write this?"

He read it, frowned, and handed it back. "Not my handwriting."

It was printed in block letters. I decided on a blunt approach. "Do you often dress up in a mummy costume?"

His features hardened. "Why are you here?"

"Renee Chastain, one of your workers, was attacked by a mummy by the riverfront two nights ago."

He chuckled in disbelief. "The mummies I work with are less animated. If it happened, it was someone else having the joke. I do not joke about ancient Egyptian history. It is my life. I'm sorry Mrs. Chastain was attacked, but surely she should not have been in that part of town at night."

I'd not said she was alone. "I understand you disapprove of her husband's poetry. Why?"

"Listen, Mr.—what is your name?"

"Frankenstein. I'm a detective."

"Do you investigate me?"

"I'm investigating the note."

"If you don't understand why I object to a husband publishing details intimate about his wife, I can add nothing. I make my feelings clear to Renee. She disagrees. Someday she will say I am right. However, she does good work and has my respect, though it's a shame her husband can't offer much support."

My dislike of the man spurred me on. "Why would a lover of Egyptian antiquity take offense to her husband's poetry? Weren't women often immodestly dressed in ancient drawings?"

He waved his hand in dismissal. "Roman statues show men and women unclothed, but that didn't mean Romans walked the streets naked. Sculptors didn't put their own wives on display."

"I suppose you're right." I sniffed.

"Any other questions," he asked.

"That's a distinctive cologne you wear."

He seemed embarrassed. "There's nothing pleasant about human smell."

I nodded and thanked him for his time. As I left Omari's office, I bumped into the man I'd seen with his arms around Renee. He was about the same height as Omari, but more muscular. He wore his dark hair long, his bangs reaching his thick eyebrows.

"Come with me, please," he said. Not used to being ordered around, I was confused, but I followed him.

His office was larger than Omari's but windowless, the walls lined with bookcases, mostly notebooks. He shut the door and sat behind his neat desk.

"My name is Alvin Marchard, one of the owners of the museum. Renee Chastain told me that you're a detective and you helped her a few days ago. I want you to prove Omari assaulted her," he said, his voice shaking. Clearly, he had an emotional investment in Renee.

"You're hiring me?" I asked.

"Yes."

It was what I had wanted to do, anyway. "All right. How long has Omari been working here?" I asked.

"About a year," he said.

"Did you do a background check before hiring him?"

"An extensive one, as we have valuable items in the museum. But there was little to find. He had just moved from Cairo. He claims to be a descendent of a pharaoh."

"What was his work history like?" I asked.

"He didn't have one. He said he was independently wealthy and had never held a real job. I told him he probably wouldn't be interested in this position, as it doesn't pay much. He didn't care. He just wanted to work in a place that appreciated Egypt's cultural heritage."

"You do have an impressive collection of Egyptian artifacts."

"Most of that came from Omari. Before he joined us, we had just a few artifacts and an ancient Egyptian mummy. Evidence tied the latter to the Pharoah Khufu, from the fourth dynasty, which would make it 4000 years old."

"I didn't notice that," I said.

"That's because someone stole it, about two months before I met Omari. He told us he owned many artifacts, some of which he would be happy to let us display, *if* we hired him. He boasted of contacts with other collectors. He also had the money to buy a fifty percent ownership in the museum." He shrugged. "We couldn't say no to such an offer."

I left thinking the Musee Histoire, like most museums, told me about the past but not about the present. Either Omari was pretending he didn't know me, or someone else had dressed up as a mummy, attacked Renee, and tried to implicate Omari with the note and perfume. Marchard was the right height, but why would he do it? Why would *anyone*? Or had Renee hired someone to attack her? Again, why? I sent Renee a letter mentioning the anonymous note I'd received and apologizing for my intrusion at her place of work. For a week I left it at that, until I received a note from Renee, begging me to come quickly to her apartment.

•   •   •

"I've seen him—the mummy—outside my window the past two nights," said Renee as she let me in. Though her rooms were modest, the walls featured some landscape paintings by artists I didn't recognize. This time she had her hood off, revealing brunette hair that reached her slim waist.

"Did he try to come in?"

"No. I think he just wanted to make sure I saw him."

"Have you or Marchard confronted Omari?"

"We both have. He just denies everything. He hates Alvin. I'm afraid of what he might do."

Before she could elaborate, we were interrupted by a lugubrious moan from the bedroom, followed by coughing.

"Excuse me," she whispered, and went to what I assumed was her husband's side. I sat for five minutes in her kitchen/dining room, waiting. It was Spartan but clean. If her husband was bedridden, he probably didn't track much mud around. I saw no evidence of children. At the other end of the table lay pieces of paper and a pencil. One of the sheets had verse on it. The writing was large and clear. I had seen it before.

When she returned, she apologized. "My husband is asleep now. Sometimes the pain is intolerable."

"What's wrong with him?"

"Consumption. His lungs are very weak. I don't know if ..." but she couldn't finish.

"Does he still write poetry? I pointed at the unfinished verse on the table.

"Physically, writing tires him, so I am his scribe and editor. It's frustrating as he's trying to finish what we believe will be his best collection. Though his body is weak, his mind has been sharpened by the pain. We just hope he is able to finish it."

I stayed with her for nearly two hours, but the mummy didn't reappear. I offered to sit with her for a few nights. She insisted she didn't have the money for that. I said she could pay after her husband had recovered, though we both knew that was unlikely to happen.

The next morning, I went to a bookseller and bought a small collection of poems by Thomas Chastain. While not an expert, I'd read my share of Coleridge, Wordsworth, and Byron. Chastain's concerns were typical of Romantic poets: nature, death, love, ancient Greece, all with an unhealthy dose of angst. I am an expert on angst, Victor having been an archetype.

In my humble opinion, Chastain's lines flowed, and he came up with impressive turns of phrase, though, to me, his writing was indistinguishable from run-of-the-mill Romantic verse. In truth, I had always been conflicted with Romantic poetry's beneficent portrayal of nature. Having ventured to the Arctic in my final confrontation with Victor Frankenstein, I had seen nature in its primal state, which is destructive and unforgiving. To survive, humanity must subdue rather than commune with nature, a battle Thomas Chastain was losing.

Igor kept late hours, so it wasn't until noon that I went to his room and told him to watch Omari in the evening from outside his house. I then went to the department of records.

I discovered Omari had lived by the lake in a rich part of the city for the past year. He was unmarried and owned his house. He must have come from wealth because there was no way he could have bought it on his museum salary. I found no trace of what he'd done before that year. I would ask him, but I figured I'd get more answers from another source.

•   •   •

A smoldering cigarette hung from Sheriff Jean Beaulieu's mouth as we sat in his office. A trim salt and pepper beard outlined the lower half of his face. He had a faint scar under his right eye that I tried not to look at. God knows, I had a few.

"The museum break-in was the kind of crime I most detest," he said. "The kind that I don't solve."

"I know the feeling."

"There was no evidence of forced entry. Not at the entrance, nor in the glass case that housed the mummy. But everyone at the museum had alibis, except for the night watchman. All he had were excuses."

"Which were?"

"He fell asleep on duty and didn't hear a thing. At first, I suspected him, but he'd never broken the law before, and he had a weakness for drink. If he did commit the crime, he didn't benefit from it. Within a month, we found his body in the river. There was another detail that made me doubt he did it."

"What was that?" I asked.

"The glass case that housed the mummy was smashed from the inside."

"How is that possible?"

"The watchman had a key, which he, or more likely, someone else could have used. Or ..." he smirked and added, "the mummy smashed the glass and carried off half a room full of artifacts."

"Maybe he did get up and walk away," I said. "Maybe someone chanted Egyptian mumbo-jumbo and brought the mummy to life."

Beaulieu shook his head. "Even if that were possible, it would have to involve someone else. The mummy couldn't do its own reanimation chant."

"I don't know," I said. "If we're going to believe in a reanimation chant, why couldn't we believe in a spell that had been made in the past to take effect on a certain date?"

Beaulieu shook his head. "Because once we start believing anything is possible, logic goes out the window, and we have nothing to work with."

•   •   •

I wanted to talk to Omari again in his office, but when I arrived, Marchard said he was out interviewing a recently returned archeologist. "You can probably catch him late in the afternoon, or later. He keeps late hours. As do I."

I thanked him. If they both kept late hours at the museum, when would they have time to stalk Renee Chastain? I went home and took a nap, intending to spend the night outside Renee's flat.

After sunset I found a pine tree about a hundred feet from the front of the Chastains' cottage. I smoothed the ground and leaned against the knotty trunk. The July evening was mild. Had I been a Romantic poet, I could have written several poems about the crickets.

Shortly after I arrived, Renee lit a candle in her kitchen. She extinguished it an hour later. If the mummy meant to scare her, he would have to wake her. I walked around the house, but not too close. There were few stars out and no moon, so I couldn't see very well. I tripped over a tree root and just caught my balance when I stepped onto something else: the supine body of a mummy!

The unexpected weight of my foot caused the body to yelp and scramble to its feet. I clamped onto its right arm before it could get any further. With a knife I cut one of the bandages around his head and pulled. It had impressive adhesive qualities, producing more yelps from the mummy. After a few unwinds, I exposed the familiar bristle haircut and thin mustache of Het Omari.

"This is what we detectives like to call *caught in the act*," I said.

Omari sputtered and fingered his raw face. "Where am I?"

"I'll answer that question if you answer mine. We're in back of Renee Chastain's house."

"What are we doing here?"

"That's the question *you're* going to answer."

"How did I get covered in bandages?"

This was not going well. "I suppose you're going to say you never before dressed up as a mummy?"

"Why would I?"

"I'm going to get an answer out of you if we have to stay here all night. What's the last thing you remember?"

He thought. "I work late in my office. The museum was closed. The only other person in building was Marchard. He says he'll make me a cup of coffee, which I accept. He brings in two, one for himself. We talk for a few moments. He has some insulting ideas for advertising my department. I tell him I will think about it, though I won't. The next thing I know, you step on me."

"You're accusing Marchard of putting a drug into your coffee, wrapping you up as a mummy, and dumping your body in back of Mrs. Chastain's house?"

"I can't think of a more—how do you say?—plausible explanation."

"I can't think of a *less* plausible one."

"Marchard wants me locked up so he can keep my Egyptian treasures."

"You're lending them to the museum. Why would he get them?"

Omari didn't have an answer for that. Instead, he yanked off a bandage that stuck to his chin. He had the kind of indignation and arrogance that either gave credence to the most ridiculous statements or made you want to kick him in the nether parts. He hadn't stolen anything. He hadn't caused Renee any physical injury. Though he might have scared her, he made no effort to enter her house.

"I guess the only thing we can do is wish Mrs. Chastain goodnight," I said, grabbing him by the arm and dragging him to the front door.

"What if she's sleeping?" he said. "This is not the time—"

After three series of knocks, and my sonorous voice, the door opened, revealing Renee in a nightgown. I brandished my evidence. "Mrs. Chastain, I found this gentleman behind your house. I recommend reporting him to the authorities."

"Renee," said Omari, his red face contrasting with the white bandages. "I know this looks bad, but I've been set up." When I let go of him, he tried to reassert his dignity by standing straight and brushing his shoulders. "I will go now. The truth will appear." He dashed away.

I explained what had happened. Renee listened incredulously. "Why is he doing this?"

"We will find out," I said.

•   •   •

Around noon the next day Igor staggered into my office. His long hair looked like a bowl shot with arrows. His smudged shirt was wrinkled, and so was my nose from his rank smell.

"Did you forget to bathe this year?" I asked.

"The year is young," he said. "Do you want to hear about Omari, or would you rather criticize my ablutions?"

"Tell me about Omari. I can criticize your ablutions any time."

"He has an impressive house, especially for someone who lives alone. Two stories, eight rooms. I couldn't get in, though. He locks all his windows. I made myself comfortable, which wasn't easy because he has a very poor lawn. A lot of bald patches. The one bush I could find to hide behind was on a slope. He came home late, around midnight."

I told him about my more interesting evening catching Omari stalking Renee in his mummy suit.

He shook his head. "Some people have a problem. What time did you stumble over him?"

"Around ten. He insists Marchard drugged and dumped him, but I never heard a cart, and I got there around 8:30. So if Marchard dumped him, it had to be before that. Omari said he was working late at the museum, but I forgot to ask him how late."

Renee did report Omari to the sheriff. Beaulieu interviewed not only him but me as well. Omari was warned to stay away from the Chastain house. He kept insisting that Marchard had drugged his coffee.

Marchard told the sheriff the coffee had been Omari's idea and that if anyone's cup had been tampered with, it was Marchard's. By the time the authorities checked, Marchard's cup had been cleaned. Omari, suspecting foul play, had left his cup on his desk. Tests revealed traces of potassium bromide. Marchard insisted that Omari could have added the drug after he drank it. No action was taken.

•　　　•　　　•

Five days after I found Omari outside the Chastain house, another woman was attacked in the city by a mummy. This woman, a prostitute, was badly beaten but survived. She received treatment at the hospital and was released. Like Renee, she'd noted the telltale scent. Omari was arrested. To my surprise, he asked to talk to me.

My profession made me no stranger to the Geneva jail. Despite this, I was filled with dread whenever I stepped into that dark, depressing building. A certain amount of style went into most municipal structures, but the architect of the jail must have felt it would be wasted on criminals. The walls were plain and thick, the windows small, and the bars in the cells unforgiving. I knew had I not mastered my hatred, I could be rotting on the wrong side of those bars.

As I walked into the room where outsiders could talk to prisoners, Omari sat lost in thought, his elbows spread on a plain wooden table.

"I thought Switzerland a tolerant country, but it has a bias against Egyptians," said Omari. "But if the sheriff doesn't like the evidence of drug in my cup, I give him more."

"Sounds like you did, with your cologne."

"You think I'm an idiot? If I was going to attack someone, why would I keep wearing it? Marchard is framing me!"

"So, what do you want from me?"

"Go to Marchard's house. It takes a lot of bandages to wrap a mummy. Check his home when no one's there. You'll find what I need. Now is the perfect time. His family is on vacation in Cologny."

It was a conflict of interest for me, but I said I'd pass on his tip to Beaulieu. "There's one thing I don't understand, Omari," I added "If you love Egypt so much, why are you here?"

He looked pained and shrugged. "Egypt is not Egypt today. Young people have lost the old values. I should stay there and fight, but I just get laughed at. When I have figured a way to gain their attention, I will return."

It struck me that Omari's view of his homeland was just as romanticized as Costain's about nature.

Beaulieu sent a man to Marchard's home. In the basement, under a table, he found the bloody bandages. Marchard said he had no idea how they got there. He was arrested, and Omari was released.

•   •   •

I didn't know what to think about this case except that I didn't like it. Renee liked it even less. During her lunch break she stormed into my office, almost tripping over my outstretched legs.

"Are you going to stand for this?" she asked, pacing in front of my desk.

"You're referring to Alvin Marchard's arrest?"

"Omari put those bandages there!"

"That *is* possible," I said. "How is Omari treating you?"

"He's gone crazy. He's started telling me I'm the spitting image of an ancient Egyptian queen. He insists that I have an Egyptian heritage."

"Do you?"

"No! My mother is French. My father is Swiss. Omari says I should wear period clothing in the Egyptian room. He wants me to come over to his house and model it."

I didn't like the sound of that. "Do you think he set up Marchard because he is jealous?"

"All I know is the wrong person is in jail."

I felt the answer lay in Omari's past. We had only his word that he was related to a rich family in Cairo. He had appeared out of nowhere, shortly after a theft. Could *he* have been the thief, creating his own opening, and then filling it with—with what? He didn't bring back the stolen item, but perhaps he sold it and bought others. It seemed the only person who could give answers was Omari. He wouldn't give them to me, but he might give them to Renee.

•   •   •

Renee was not thrilled about modeling ancient Egyptian outfits at her home, but I convinced her it was our best bet to get Omari to say something incriminating. Igor and I would hide in Renee's bedroom, where I drilled two small holes in the wall so we could watch.

It was the first time either of us had seen her ailing husband. The drugs had left him asleep, his chest rattling. Though barely 30, his graying hair hung limp like dead grass, and his face was lined and white. The hand that had written of nature's beneficence lay open across his heart like a claw. I tried not to think of him as we sat on wooden chairs Renee had provided us.

Omari arrived exactly at 7 p.m., nattily dressed in a white shirt and narrow tie. He carried a large bag, which contained the period dress. Renee offered him something to drink, but he declined, sitting at the dining room table.

"I am surprised to be here," he said. "When I mentioned this subject before, your rejections were clear. What changed your mind?"

"As a married woman, I didn't think it proper to go to your home, but when you agreed to come here, while my husband was present, I thought it was acceptable. Plus, anything that increases interest in the museum makes my job more secure."

Omari frowned. "I was so eager that you try on these clothes that I didn't think. Your caution commends you. How is your husband doing?"

She shook her head. "Stable, but no better."

"I'm sorry. Though I don't approve of his writing, I wish him no ill. So, are you ready to try on the clothing?"

"Yes. How old is it?"

"Not old, except in style. These are copies of ancient clothes."

He opened his bag and pulled out a white dress with shoulder straps, a tan shawl, a black wig with a skullcap, and a cone for the top of the head. She excused herself to get dressed in her bedroom. As we were in there, she'd set up a curtain for privacy. She emerged looking like Cleopatra. Igor and I were impressed, but not as much as Omari, whose widened eyes and open mouth revealed his love for her.

"You are the image of Queen Sobekneferu," he said, breathless.

She laughed nervously. "How can you know that? I thought the only statues extent of her are headless."

"Well, that is true, but there are descriptions. You match her in beauty and bearing."

"So, you want me to wear this outfit at the museum?"

"Not exactly. Tell me, Renee, if I may call you that. Have you thought of what you will do after your husband … is gone?"

Renee stiffened. "I cannot think of such things."

"Of course. But preparation is best." When she didn't respond, he continued. "I come from an old Egyptian family and own a number of priceless artifacts, enough so that we live well for the rest of our lives."

"In Geneva?"

"No. Only in Egypt would you be recognized for the queen that you are. With you at my side, we could put that country back on its path to greatness."

I feared Renee would get angry and throw him out of the house. Despite his implied connection to Queen Sobekneferu, to this point he'd said nothing we could use against him. I wanted to know more about his artifacts. To get her attention, I knocked over a book, causing it to crash to the floor.

"Oh, my husband is awake!" she said.

Omari backed from her. "Perhaps I must go."

Renee's eyes flashed. "Wait. You speak of going to Egypt. It seems so far away."

"Not so far. We could reach Genoa in week, then a ship takes us to Alexandria."

After a pause, she asked, "Have you heard anything new about Mr. Marchard?"

"His trial starts Thursday. You must forget about that."

Another book crashed to the floor, this time unintentionally, as Igor knocked it over with his back. Omari jumped out of his chair.

"Either your husband needs you or your library is falling. Thank you. We will talk tomorrow."

"What about these clothes?"

"Bring them to the museum tomorrow."

With that, he nodded and walked out of the house. Renee rushed into the bedroom. "I am afraid that was a waste of time."

I reached out to pat her on the shoulder, but as it was exposed, I pulled my hand back. "Maybe not. We know what he plans to do, and he mentioned he had priceless artifacts, which he may have stolen from the museum."

I gave the tip to Beaulieu. He checked out Omari's home but found nothing incriminating. If Omari had robbed the museum, it wouldn't be easy for him to sell his ill-gotten gains. If I were Omari, where would I hide them?

Before I could answer that question, Thomas Chastain died.

•   •   •

The funeral was a small affair, reflecting Chastain's readership. Among those in attendance were Igor, me, and Omari. I felt sorry for the Romantic poet as he was lowered into the ground and returned to nature.

I kept in contact with Renee but could do little for her. Thomas's death emboldened Omari. Every day she had to rebuff his suggestions that they take their relationship to the next step.

She hoped that her husband's final book of poetry would sour Omari. The day it came out, she handed me a copy. Looking it over, I noticed a poem called "Intersection." It took place in a museum and commented on the past's pull on the present. It seemed innocuous enough until I came to this line: *"Small-minded men would dress their idealized women / in rags of the past, trying to capture a moment forever lost."*

I held up the book and asked, "How much of this did you write?"

Her body wavered like a toppling tree. "All of it."

"Good. I have an idea that might get Omari off your back."

News in the press travels slowly, but even small items, if properly placed, can grow like a rolling snowball. After a week or so, everyone aware of Thomas Chastain knew that his final collection, *Distant Influences*, was written by his wife.

Renee was reluctant to confirm this, fearing it would tarnish her husband's reputation, but I told her if art is the pursuit of truth, it cannot be based on a lie. Also, she had a gift, and if she wished to continue using it, she could no longer hide under her husband's name. Even if she used a pseudonym, the similarity in style would eventually be traced. When she publicly admitted authorship, the reaction was mixed. One critic accused her of plagiarizing from Thomas and insisted a woman could not have written such verse. One praised her for broadening the scope of Romantic poetry. Most people ignored the book completely.

The effect on Omari was as I hoped. Appalled that Renee had written such indecorous verse, he insisted she print a retraction. She laughed and told him she wouldn't rest until he was in jail instead of Marchard. He said her trafficking in Romantic poetry had addled her senses.

It was another poem, "Dust to Dust," about someone passing on, from Chastain's point of view, that gave me the final clue. One of its points was that, in the end, everyone ended up in the earth with nature. That didn't exactly comfort me until I realized that eventually the earth claimed not only everyone but every *thing*.

Igor had said Omari's lawn had lots of bald spots. Could that be because he'd buried the stolen artifacts there and couldn't resist looking at them from time to time? The next morning, I had Igor go to the museum with instructions to confirm that Omari was there.

I soon received two messages. Igor wrote: "He's not here, today or yesterday." At the bottom were words from Renee: "Please come to the museum as soon as possible."

When I arrived, a confused Renee and an irritable Igor directed me to Omari's office, where Beaulieu waited. Lying on the floor in front of Omari's desk was a full-length mummy. It looked and smelled authentic.

"Omari must have buried this in his yard," I said. "We need to go there now." Beaulieu picked up a sheet of paper lying across the desk and handed it to me. "Read this first."

It was from Omari.

"I have decided the 19th century and I are incompatible. Even if Mrs. Chastain is a descendant of an ancient Egyptian queen, her environment has made her unworthy to be my mate. For those reasons, I have re-uttered the animation spell and reversed its effects. You see the results before you. I have made arrangements so that I will be revived a thousand years hence. Perhaps that time will be more civilized than this one. I leave my future in your hands."

I looked at the mummy. It seemed smaller and thinner than the man I knew.

"We're supposed to believe this is Omari?" I asked.

"I don't know about that, but it looks similar to the mummy stolen one and a half years ago," said Renee. "It would explain a lot of things."

"It explains too many things," I said. "Check and see if anything is missing from the museum. Igor, we need to get to his house immediately."

"If I were him," said Beaulieu, holding his smoldering pipe, "I'd do whatever I had to do at my home before I left a mummy in my office. Any idea where he might go?"

"Back to Egypt, via Genoa," I said.

"He's probably already left. If he's carrying heavy artifacts, he's in a horse cart. We could catch him on horseback if we go *now*."

"How can we know which road he took?" I asked.

Beaulieu smiled. "If he's in a hurry, there's only one way."

Beaulieu said he would go to Omari's house, as he couldn't just leave Geneva. Igor and I would chase Omari on horseback. If there was no word of him passing through after a couple of days, we would turn back. Neither Igor nor I were accomplished horsemen, but at least Igor was light. My horse must have felt the Golem had mounted him.

After about 20 miles we started asking at inns if Omari had stopped there. At the 30-mile mark we got confirmation. Our final assist was from the weather. Though Igor complained that if he drowned from the rain I'd have to pay him double, we were both cheered to find Omari's horse cart stuck in the mud. Omari was shouting imprecations at the driver, who tried to urge the horse forward.

"We'd be happy to help," I said. "But in payment, I'm afraid we'd insist on you changing your direction."

"Frankenstein," said Omari, his voice resigned. "I'm sorry you didn't believe that the mummy I left was me. I poured myself into making it."

"So that mummy was a fake, just like you," I said.

Drenched and splattered, he looked more like a mud baby than an Egyptian scholar, yet he retained an equanimity that impressed me. "My devotion to my culture is true."

"You're just a thief who uses his knowledge of antiquity to prey on vulnerable people like Mrs. Chastain."

"She doesn't know who she is. With her by my side in Cairo, we could have done anything."

"In Geneva, your options are going to be more limited."

Return transportation required some juggling. Igor had to stay with the horse cart. Omari and I took two days to ride back to Geneva's prison.

An inventory of the Egyptian room revealed that Omari had made replicas of a number of smaller, more portable artifacts, including a papyrus, a necklace, and some rings, and stolen the originals. He was also charged with attacking the prostitute and falsely implicating Marchard, who was released with apologies.

In Igor's room we talked about what had transpired.

"Not that I expect mummy dressers to make sense," said Igor, "but if he had lots of money, why work at the museum? Why set up Marchard? Why risk everything to make an offer to Renee?"

"He worked at the museum because he loved Egyptian culture. He also was obsessed with Renee and thought she could help him reassume what he thought was his proper place in Egyptian society. But he had to get rid of Marchard. Ultimately, he was an exile looking for a place to belong. I can identify with that," I said.

"What are you an exile from?"

"Victor Frankenstein's idea of the perfect man."

Omari was found guilty of all charges. He later sent me a note saying, *Stay true to your heritage.* Unless he was implying that Egyptians were thieves, I didn't see how he was living up to his own advice. But as I thought about it, I realized we were all thieves.

The Romantic poets glorified our relationship with nature, but the truth was, we killed animals and plants to survive. I was the product of someone else's dead body parts, trying to steal a better life than the one I'd been given. In time, we would all be caught.

7

Wherefore Art Thou, Werewolf

I HAVE A RECURRING NIGHTMARE where I think I'm suffocating—you might too if you had electrodes protruding from both sides of your neck. I wake up gasping, then realize it was only a dream. Except this time, it wasn't.

A hairy, long-nailed claw clasped my throat. I kicked up my right leg, producing a growling grunt and more importantly, freeing my windpipe. I then delivered a head butt, an effective maneuver as my flat skull has a large area of contact. A heavy weight crashed to the floor. I rolled off the other side of my bed.

"Who are you?" I demanded.

"Rowwrlll!" it said.

Keeping my eyes on the hairy, dazed mass, I feverishly lit my hurricane lamp. The fluttering light revealed a large, muscular brute, its body covered with fur. "Wolf Man" escaped my lips. A blast of December air from the open window told me how he got in.

"Why did you attack me?" I asked, though I was unsure if Wolf Men could speak human dialogue.

"Not attack. Wake. Need help." He spit out his words.

"What kind of help?"

"Need find dead body of Milosh, bring to life, put curse back."

"Who's Milosh?"

The Wolf Man sat upright on the floor, looking slightly more human. "Gypsy son who put werewolf curse on Heinz Bauer."

"You're Heinz Bauer?"

"Yes ... and no."

I hated those kinds of answers.

"Why do you want this Milosh brought back to life?"

His large body shook. "His nightmare over. Mine monthly. You bring him back to life. I reinfect."

I sat on my armchair, which groaned under my weight. "You have me confused with Victor Frankenstein. I assumed his last name for publicity purposes. But I did not inherit his medical expertise. He's also dead, his body frozen in the Arctic."

"You have his papers."

I shook my head. "The fireplace has them."

"Victor had assistant?"

"Igor? For surgery, I wouldn't trust him to pull my leg."

"I visit."

"Stay away from him."

"I desperate." From his torn pants pocket he spilled a handful of coins onto the floor. "Find Milosh's body. I return in month."

With that, he leapt out the window and vanished, his loping footfalls echoing in the night. There were only three hours left until dawn. If he found Igor in that time, he was a better detective than I.

Perhaps my blighted past had numbed my nerves, but somehow I fell asleep after all that. In the morning I awoke to a tipped-over bookcase, a gouged nightstand with open drawers, tufts of fur, and a foul animal odor. After cleaning up, I brewed some strong tea and ruminated.

How had such a crazed, tormented being found me? Would he even remember to return? I could let nature take its course, but the irony of someone artificially resurrected from dead body parts doing that was too much, even for me. I decided to look for Heinz Bauer.

Someone who turned into a murderous werewolf once a month would probably attempt a low profile the other twenty-nine or thirty days. Fortunately, when the creature emptied his pockets to pay me, he'd accidentally left a soiled handkerchief, a small key, and a rent receipt. Though the receipt contained no address, it was signed by Anna Holbein.

I tracked her to a rundown house on the north end of Geneva. No one answered my knock, but the key fit the lock just fine.

The interior was simple, neat, and dark. All the doors were ajar except one at the end of a hallway. I pulled it open, revealing a room not much bigger than a closet, almost all of it taken up with prostrate Heinz Bauer sprawled on a disheveled bed. When I shook his shoulder, he turned over. His face was raked with scratches, but no blood. Perhaps I was his only encounter last night. I held up his key.

"I appreciate the gesture, but we hardly know each other," he said.

He didn't even flinch at the sight of my seven-foot frame. Instead, he moaned, palming his head as if it were a coconut.

"Mrs. Holbein didn't appreciate it when she had to let me in at 5 a.m."

I placed the key on his nightstand. "Do you remember coming to my room last night?"

"I do." His haunted eyes blazed in confirmation.

"You wanted me to find and reanimate the body of someone named Milosh. What's that all about?"

He let out a sigh that could have registered in a hot-air balloon. "Ten years ago, Milosh Salazar attacked a woman in the woods. I intervened and killed him, but not before he bit and infected me."

"You've lived with it this long?"

He nodded. "I likened my transformations to monthly drinking bouts where I temporarily lost control. The morning after, I felt flattened and humiliated but swore to continue fighting. Then six months ago my parents discovered my secret, and I ..." His voice broke. "I killed them."

"You or the Wolf Man killed them?"

He laughed, without mirth. "The line between us has been blurred. Though the Wolf Man is dominant only one night a month, we are never completely separated. Sometimes, in human form, I do inexplicable things at his influence, while his visit to you last night was partially my intention."

"Why me?"

"I heard about you, that you've accepted and used your monstrousness to your advantage as a detective. Like the Wolf Man, you were roiled by an uncontrollable anger against your creator. Yet, you overcame it."

"By killing him, indirectly."

"But you now pity him. Anger makes the Wolf Man kill. If he could see Milosh as a kindred spirit, it could be a first step toward the fiend developing empathy and overcoming his need to kill. Milosh's mother is still alive. Afternoons and evenings she and about fifteen other gypsies sell goods near the lake. We could talk to her, get a sense of her dead son as a tragic human being, and eventually the Wolf Man. What do you think?"

I thought it was rubbish. A kinder, gentler Wolf Man might ask, "Would you like your throat ripped or your head bashed in?" But you'd still end up dead. Then again, my anger had been tamed by music and the sight of a child.

"If you wanted my services, why didn't you just come as Heinz Bauer?"

His body sagged. "I have spent most of my adult life denying the evil within me, but the fiend's influence has only grown. I was afraid to seek you out because all of this might bring me closer to the abyss. The Wolf Man, however, fears nothing. If you're wondering where you fit in, I need someone who understands and can offer protection. Gypsies have long memories. Members of the Salazar family would like me dead." He added, "I did pay you, after all."

Unable to turn my back on a fellow monster in need, I took the case. I just hoped I didn't get bitten by an infected wolf. I could see the next potboiler: "Frankenstein *is* the Wolf Man."

That evening we found the gypsies' wagon, parked near the port on the southern edge of Lake Geneva, where they sold Romani clothes, arts, and crafts. In addition, some gypsies performed fast-paced folk songs on a Flamenco guitar, violin, and an old jug. A young woman with long black hair and native outfit danced. The mood was festive, and alcohol flowed freely.

Bauer pointed out a much older woman seated behind a table of gypsy apparel, her gray hair wrapped in a bandana, her eyes combing the audience for customers. In contrast to the others, she appeared solemn and all business. I suggested talking to her right there, but Bauer insisted we track them to their after-hour location, then talk. He was the client.

The crowd cleared around eleven, the gypsies packed up their gear into their wagon, and at a discreet distance, we followed them. They led us to the outskirts of town, in a northeasterly direction, two miles from the port. There they stopped.

Now that we had found their camp, Bauer advocated a direct approach. Leery of what the young Romani men might do after drinking wine all night, I advised caution. We waited until all the gypsies were setting up tents in front of us, then approached the old woman. The gypsies froze at the sight of us.

"You!" she said, glaring at Bauer.

"Florika Salazar, I know I'm the last person you expected to see ..." Bauer said.

"Someone should do to you what you did to my son," the gypsy hissed, then picked up a fallen branch and started hitting my client over the head with it. Bauer warded off the blows with his arms. I glanced at the wall of gypsies, but they just watched, perhaps used to their matriarch's anger. I let her expend some energy, then pulled her off. She looked at me, then her stick, and dropped it to the ground.

"Old gypsy saying: He who beats tree with its own branch might as well spit in the ocean," she said.

One of the things holding back gypsies was their sayings.

"We are here because Heinz Bauer has a problem," I said.

She snorted. "He's the man who cries wolf every time he says his name."

"His problem is your problem. When there's a full moon, he is filled with anger that focuses on your son."

"Heinz Bauer can do nothing to my son now."

"We know that, but he wants to restore Milosh to life and re-infect him."

"He's nuts. What you want from me? Recommend asylum?"

"No. We want to defuse his anger. We wish to learn all we can about Milosh to convince the Wolf Man that his tragic life deserves sympathy rather than hate."

She looked at us with suspicion. "What you want to know?"

"I'd like you to conduct a séance so we could talk to your son directly," Bauer said.

"What you think I am? Postal service to the dead? They do not like to be disturbed. Are you even believers?"

Bauer insisted he was. I was a man of science—if not for science I wouldn't be a man at all—but in deference to the pursuit of knowledge, I maintained an open mind.

"Just one thing," Bauer said. "I'm very busy the next few weeks. Could we do this on the 17th of next month?"

Florika's eyes widened, and so did mine. "You want a séance on that night?" Her breath came out like air from a bellows. "We can do that."

After we walked away, I said, "What's the idea ..." Then I figured it out. "There's a full moon that night."

"This won't work unless the Wolf Man gets the information directly."

"Oh, and he's going to intellectually process this information and become a monk? What's to stop Florika's sons from filling you with silver bullets?"

"Then my problems will be solved."

"Wonderful. Now why don't you tell me how she knew you?"

He looked up at the star-less sky, then back at me. "After I was first infected, I approached her."

"And she was unsympathetic?"

"She said nothing could be done, then her family disappeared. For years I thought, good riddance, but after I killed my parents, I thought only she could help me. Five weeks ago, they returned to Geneva. This will work, or it won't, but either way, it will be resolved."

It was a dilemma. Unlike gypsies, the Frankenstein family had only one saying: "*What* have I done?" which covered the sins of omission as well as commission. I would accompany Bauer to his séance.

In the meantime, I pursued less monstrous cases. The bearded lady at the circus suspected her trapeze artist husband of swinging beyond the safety net of their marriage. I caught him sticking it to the sword swallower.

A man bought a pearl necklace that turned out to be fake and wanted someone to lean on the seller for a refund. The sight of my face inches from the transgressor did the trick. My unusual height helped with another assignment, to get Frau Kirshner's cat out of a tree.

The afternoon of the next full moon, Bauer and I walked toward the gypsy camp. It didn't surprise me that their market stall closed early that day. Clouds drifted across the twilit sky, while a faint breeze animated the woods.

"I'm assuming it doesn't matter if we don't see the full moon," I said.

"It takes more than clouds to stop this," Bauer said, his face grim. "It won't be long."

"How does it feel, to change?"

"To lose the sanctity of one's own skin is terrifying, but worse is the gradual merging of wolf and man. My morality has become fluid. I need you to ensure some stability." He handed me a pistol. I held it like a dead weasel.

"I rarely use these."

"The silver bullets inside could come in handy."

I reluctantly pocketed the pistol. We trudged a few minutes more.

"Do you ever ask yourself *why?*" he asked.

I shrugged. "Everybody does. Eventually, you realize it's better to ask, 'Now what?'"

He nodded. "I agree."

A mile from the gypsy camp I heard a savage growl. I turned and saw Bauer convulsed in pain.

"Time to put your kid gloves away," he said, hair sprouting from the unwilling garden of his flesh. His skull widened, his hands lost their definition, and his body curled like an ape's. His arms crossed over his face, but he couldn't ward off what was already inside him. The hairy arms dropped, and the slobbering jaws of the Wolf Man jutted toward me.

"Are you all right, Bauer?" It was one of the most ridiculous questions I've ever asked.

"Let's go," he growled.

I wondered how much of Bauer was there, but I doubted even he knew. Choices were hard enough without having to deal with conflicting ideas of right and wrong. I led the way, slowing our progress with many backward glances.

Three burly male gypsies, each with pistols, met us at the edge of an open field. With calm deliberation they escorted us to a small round table set in front of their wagons. Florika sat flanked by two other chairs. A simple candle flickered in the center.

"Sit," she said. The Wolf Man growled but obeyed, her guards wrapping chains around him, then standing behind us.

"Have either of you participated in a séance before?" I said no, while the Wolf Man grunted. "I guarantee nothing. I cannot make contact with an unwilling spirit." She glared at me. "No refund though."

"I understand." At this point I just wanted to get through the séance without anyone dying.

"I do this not for you, but to free my family from your hate," she said to the Wolf Man. "If we make contact, do not break the circle of hands."

I glanced at Bauer, his fur glistening, I hoped, from an effort to control himself. "We will cooperate," I said.

"Very well. Let's begin."

We joined hands, the Wolf Man's right completely obscuring Mrs. Florika's left.

She spoke to her dead son, apologizing for disturbing his rest. She explained our purpose: that the Wolf Man wanted an opportunity to confront and understand the man responsible for his infection. Finally, she pled for Milosh to speak. The Wolf Man echoed the excitement with growls of increased volume.

At some point the candle blew out, throwing us into darkness. If the gypsies intended to rid the world of the Wolf Man, this would be the time. Nothing happened, however, except Florika moaned either nonsense syllables or Romani words, her voice an octave lower than normal. I grew impatient, when abruptly she switched to French.

"You are the man who killed me. Why have you disturbed my rest?" a low voice asked. The Wolf Man hissed.

"Heinz Bauer is struggling with the werewolf curse, as you did," I said.

"There is but one escape. I was freed when you beat me with the silver walking stick. My family can offer you a less painful exit. One silver bullet and your agony will be over."

"That's not the type of freedom we are seeking," I said.

The Wolf Man leaned forward. "Where you buried?"

The spirit laughed. "In the shade of the woods, the murmur of water, in the embrace of my family, while you run tormented, above ground, with nowhere to hide."

That meant nothing to me, but at that moment the full moon broke out from behind the clouds. The Wolf Man lifted the table and crashed it against the three gypsies. They fell back while the Wolf Man's chest split the chains like noodles. He then dashed into the woods.

I pulled out my pistol and flourished it at the other gypsies pouring from their tents. I backed away, then broke into a full run for the woods.

I could only follow the Wolf Man. For five minutes I dodged tree trunks, my legs buckling against unseen rocks and holes, my less-than-handsome face raked by gnarled branches. Eventually, I came upon a smaller field, where I tripped over a tombstone.

Landing hard on my shoulder, I swore mightily, then heard a gurgling pond, a savage panting, and the sound of digging claws. I rolled to my other side and saw ten gravestones dotting the field. Next to one, thirty feet away, the Wolf Man swiped handfuls of dirt into the air.

I jumped to my feet. "Stop!" I yelled, but he ignored me. I rushed to the gravesite, but he'd already torn off the coffin lid and pulled out a skull.

What I saw next I didn't want to believe. As the full moon shone down on Milosh Salazar's skull, its outline fluttered like an echo. A shadowy light, like a candle in fog, lit up the reassembling bones. The trunk and limbs filled out.

The Wolf Man shook the corpse as would a tiger with a helpless deer in its mouth. Except this deer wasn't helpless. With each shake it got longer, broader, more defined, until I heard the slap of a hairy open fist. The Wolf Man lost his grip, while reborn Milosh scrambled to his feet. The two werewolves circled each other, swiping and snarling like living hatred.

"Heinz, back away from him!" I warned, but neither listened. I raised my pistol.

Bauer threw me a baleful glance. "Just spare him."

Milosh leaped at his foe. Though I was fifteen feet away, there was no escaping the snarling, scratching, bloody blows, and screams of pain. I had no moral conflict in putting Milosh out of his misery, but could I snuff out the life of Heinz Bauer as well?

I fired into the center of the savagery that was Milosh Salazar. His death bellow filled the air as he grew limp in Bauer's grasp, then fell to the ground. Among the trees I spotted five gypsy men, guns poised.

We watched the fallen werewolf transform, the hair and skin disintegrating, leaving a decayed corpse. The surviving Wolf Man looked at me.

More shots rang out, mine and the gypsies'. As the Wolf Man hit the ground, his body transformed back to Heinz Bauer. As I loped to it, he turned to me, grimacing.

"Only my death can separate me from the werewolf, but I can live a normal life if you bring me back."

"I told you, I don't have that ability. I'm not a scientist who thinks he is God. I'm just a detective."

His last words were, "You're a functioning monster."

•　　　•　　　•

I tried to save him. I preserved his body in ice and combed the Frankenstein castle for its secrets. The tangled wires and the hideous, dust-gathering machines sat within those crumbling walls like the shards of an obscene idea. But I could not bring it or Heinz Bauer to life, for it was not my idea, nor should it be any human's. Like Bauer and the Wolf Man, it had to die with Victor Frankenstein.

8

The Sum of Its Parts

A SHORT, CRAGGY-FACED MAN in a salt-encrusted coat stood in front of the Pernell Machine Tool factory, its tiny windows looking over the area like the hundred eyes of Argus. A biting March wind cut through his clothes. Tufts of his gray beard protruded like lichen. The black night, the locked factory buildings, and the fetid smell of waste warned people away from the East London street. Not even prostitutes sold their wares in this place, which made it an ideal transactional location if one wished to be unseen. The area, unfamiliar to him, had been suggested by the buyer. If only he would turn up. Darius was anxious to sell to sell this specimen, having tired of preserving it.

He heard clomping footsteps, slow as a heartbeat, approaching. A tall figure in a hooded black cloak appeared rounding the corner. It had to be the buyer. No one else would be on this street at this time of night. The figure came to within five feet of him and stopped, its eyes clamping down on him. Darius found the silence, the figure's height, and the stillness unnerving. He had been scared many times in his life and had never enjoyed it.

"Do you want to buy something, or are you just going to stand there all night?" he asked.

"The burden of proof is on you." The voice was cold, with a harsh German accent. To his surprise, he saw it was a woman.

From within his coat he pulled out a sealed jar. "As I told you, I was the doctor on the *Rosalind*. It was the mad scientist himself on his deathbed who suggested we preserve his brain."

"How was it done?"

"We were in the Arctic, weren't we? The wind off the water freezes everything: thoughts in your head, your will to live, the passing of each day. After we reached warmer seas, I injected the brain's tissues with colored wax and kept it in this sealed jar."

"That does not prove this is *his* brain."

He reached into his pocket and pulled out a golden ring. On the band were the initials VF. He handed it to the woman, who inspected it.

"It's his ring," she said. "You probably stole it."

He felt himself losing patience. "Maybe you would like the brain to start talking to you, but that's not going to happen. I give you my word that this is the brain I extracted from the dead man's head, an act I don't intend to repeat."

"And what exactly is your word worth?"

The man's face creased, and it was already creased from many years on the sea. "How valuable is the only chance you have to get the brain of one such as he? His body is at the bottom of the Arctic Ocean. This is all that remains. If you don't want it, just say so, and stop wasting my time."

The woman laughed, dismissing the notion that Darius's time had any value. "If is it not what you say, I will find you."

He scowled. "Good luck with that. I'll even narrow your search. I'll be on one of hundreds of ships plying the seven seas. Just look for Phineas Buchanan."

"Your name is Darius Pardo. You stole the brain from Phineas Buchanan."

Darius hesitated, feeling violated by the loss of his anonymity. He'd handled this all wrong, letting her decide where and when to meet. Somehow, he had to seize control. "And who might you be?"

"Since when have you cared about the source of your coins?" She reached into her coat and held out a bag of money. That was what he had come for. The best thing he could do was take it and leave. Darius placed the jar on the ground, took the bag, and looked over its contents.

"We have a deal." He stuffed the bag into his coat and turned to go. Once he reached the corner, he broke into a run, though his lungs protested and the coins jingled. Ungainly footfalls thumped in his direction with increasing volume. This woman was a lunatic. His life had been so hard, a series of thefts and double-crosses, perpetrated by and to him. Still, he was not ready to surrender it for a sack of money.

"I'll give you the money back!" he screamed, but the footfalls only got louder, flattening the frozen ground. He kept expecting a hand to clamp down on his shoulder. He never saw the blunt object crash onto his skull nor felt the knife that sliced his throat.

•   •   •

Igor sat alone at the chipped, slanting table in Les Trois Rois tavern, staring at his half-full beer mug. He did not consider waxing philosophical a good use of time, but on occasional drunken nights, when his brain was least able to plumb the depths of speculative possibility, he did so. He was aware that such limitations simplified his life.

For instance, his hunchback precluded the possibility that any beautiful woman would want to sleep with him, but this freed him from disappointment when his suggestive banter with the barmaids met with rejection and insult. He stared at his mug, which gave him direction. He needed to empty it. Then he would have to decide whether or not to have it filled and repeat the process. He'd lost track of how many times he'd decided to go for a refill.

"Do you think I've had enough, Gerhard?"

Gerhard, a wiry, bearded man who'd lived most of his 40-year life in the German section of Switzerland, still couldn't believe he was a bartender in a dumpy Geneva tavern. His French was weak enough to make him feel like an idiot most of the time.

"Have you more money?" he asked, devoting more attention to wiping the counter than to Igor.

"Is that the basis of our relationship?"

"It's the basis of all relationships."

Igor smiled. "I will devote my life to proving you wrong." He focused his eyes on the grandfather clock to the left of the bar. "Starting tomorrow, as today is slipping through my fingers like ... my command of words." He sat back in his chair, surprised at how uncomfortable it was, despite his inebriation. His eyes followed Ines's ample hips as she strode past him to clean up the neighboring table.

"Ines, would you like a ride home tonight?"

"You don't have a horse cart."

"I wasn't talking about a horse cart."

Even with the dim lantern light and her red face, one could see her blush. "You should be ashamed of yourself, talking to a woman that way."

"It's straight talk, Ines. I'm a man, you're a woman. It's against nature to pretend this animal attraction between us doesn't exist."

"I don't need to pretend."

"Ah, once again you've crushed my world," he said, leaving her a generous tip and rising to his feet. All good things came to an end, but that was all right, as the same was true for bad things. Also, many of those things resumed the following morning, however late that day began.

Les Rois Trois was nearly empty. Three young men sat at a table, one holding court with a meandering speech, the other two on the edge of consciousness. Two other men, at separate tables, were passed out, and Igor was thankful that Frankenstein had saved him from such a pointless life.

One of his favorite parts of the evenings was the mile walk between the tavern and his rented room. Putting one foot in front of the other was often a challenge, but one that he could invariably meet, regardless of his state of intoxication. In the dark of night, his hunchback was obscured, and he could pretend that he was as normal as anyone else. In this neighborhood, at this time, that was probably true.

On clear nights he liked to look up at the stars and pick out the constellations. He always started with the Big Dipper, then the Little Dipper. Then he tried to branch out to Ursa Major. Usually, he could also find the W of Cassiopeia. Tonight, he couldn't get his bearings. The stars were out of focus and incomprehensible. Maybe he was drunker than usual. The order of the heavens would have to carry on without him.

Igor heard a scuffling and a lunge. He turned and saw a knife glisten in the starlight. He grabbed the attacker's right hand, halting the plunge of the blade. The attacker was taller than Gerhard, and strong. His hooded face and cloak covered any other body characteristics.

From out of nowhere the attacker's left fist smashed into Igor's face. As Igor's world spun, he tightened his grip and launched his knee into the attacker's groin, producing a yelp, but not loosening the knife.

"If you want to take my life, you'll have to work harder than that!" Igor gasped, bending the wrist of the knifed hand grotesquely. Another twist and the hand broke off, though it held onto the weapon. Blood spattered Igor's face as the attacker screamed, backed off, and fled. Igor pried the knife free, then wrapped the hand in his vile handkerchief. The knife he pocketed.

It is not only the *moral* fabric of the city that is falling apart, he thought as he resumed his walk home.

•   •   •

Frankenstein ducked under the doorway as he strode into the office of Sheriff Jean Beaulieu. He noticed Igor, his face bruised, sitting to the side of Beaulieu's desk. The monster turned detective had been in this room many times. Beaulieu, like a number of residents of Geneva, had turned to Frankenstein when they had a problem with monsters

"What happened to you?" he asked Igor.

"Someone objected to my existence and tried to do something about it."

"I summoned you so we could all talk about that." Beaulieu's pipe leaked a curl of smoke. His deep voice and barrel-like build exuded authority, especially next to hunchbacked Igor, though Frankenstein towered over the sheriff like a shade tree. Beaulieu and Frankenstein shook hands, then Frankenstein sat in the only other chair.

"I won't ask you to shake hands with our evidence," said Beaulieu, taking out the severed right hand wrapped in paper from his desk.

"It looked more imposing while it was attached to a body and a knife," said Igor. He then described how he had been attacked outside of Les Trois Rois.

"Ah yes," said Frankenstein. "The royalty of disreputable taverns."

Igor shrugged, which, with his hunchback was anything but a subtle movement. "Disreputable characters need to stick together."

"We, of course, examined the hand," said Beaulieu. "Other than the fact that it has no corresponding body, there is nothing extraordinary about it, except for one thing: this isn't the first time it has been separated. We noticed evidence that it had been sewn back on. Do you know anyone who could do that?"

Frankenstein sighed. "I know someone who used to be able to do that, but he is dead. It stands to reason that if one person could do it, someone else could, but I'm not aware of anyone."

"You're talking about Victor Frankenstein. Did he have any followers?" asked Beaulieu.

Frankenstein shook his head. "Other than me, to the ends of the Earth? No, Victor was a loner. His idea of happiness was immersing himself in his experiments. Working with other people would have diluted the experience. There were some professors at Ingolstadt that pointed him in the direction of creating life, but he didn't confide that sort of thing to me." Ingolstadt was 300 miles away in Germany, where Victor studied. Frankenstein turned to Igor. "Did he say anything to you?"

"Not directly, but I remember him ranting about two of his professors. One named Krempe was even more anti-social than Victor—couldn't connect with students if his life depended on it. His contempt for humanity might have helped convince Victor to try to improve on it. When Krempe found out that Victor was experimenting on corpses, the professor tried to dissuade him. Victor thought it was jealousy."

"You said two professors," said Beaulieu.

"I think the other's name was Waldman. Victor had a lower opinion of him. He referred to him as a person who had no ability to improve upon what he read, so why read at all? To Waldman, the research's importance lay only in how much fame it conferred."

"How do you know all this?" Frankenstein asked.

Igor shrugged. "Victor liked to talk, often at the expense of others. One of the values he saw in me was as a listener."

"I think I've heard of this Dr. Waldman," said Beaulieu. He went to a bookcase, pulled out a beat-up notebook, and rifled through it. He stopped at a page three-quarters into it. "I thought so. Six months ago a Klaus Waldman moved to Geneva. He currently teaches at the Academy and has ruffled some feathers. Some of his students organized a protest against him. The president of the university was going to fire him, but then suddenly changed his mind."

"What did he do to ruffle feathers?" asked Frankenstein.

"My understanding is he's incompetent, but it might just be that he asked his students to actually work and they got angry."

"I'll talk to him," said Frankenstein. "I always wanted to go to the Academy. I also have Victor's diaries. They're not my favorite reading, but they might shed some light on the two professors. I'll see what I can find there."

"Good idea," said Beaulieu. "While you're doing that, I'll focus on the attacker. We know he was tall, like you, which limits him to about one percent of the population." He turned to Igor. "You have no idea why he attacked you?"

Igor shrugged. "Many associate my hunchback with moral failings. Plus, I am a man who speaks his mind, such as it is. Most people don't want to know its contents. Half the time, neither do I."

"Do you think he was trying to kill you or rob you?" asked Beaulieu.

"I'm afraid it's a bit of a blur, except for the knife. That was sharp."

"We've had recent reports about people missing from the same part of Geneva," said Beaulieu. "One was a prostitute, the other a laborer. They could be connected. Both happened late at night. I'll talk again to the laborer's wife. You let me know what you learn about Waldman."

•   •   •

Victor believed printed words were sacred, especially his, and he filled notebooks with his thoughts, plans, theories, and experiments. Fortunately for Frankenstein, he largely kept them in separate notebooks, four of them spanning his two years at Ingolstadt. In one of them Frankenstein located a passage describing the first meeting between Victor and professor Krempe. The initial impression was not positive.

"I seem to have been living with a misunderstanding about professors," Victor wrote. "I thought their primary purpose was to inspire their students to better themselves. But I left the office of Dr. Krempe, the professor of Natural History, feeling deflated and defeated. Kempe is a squat, unkempt man with a brusque manner who lives for his studies. Though in his 30s, he seems older, lacking the energy and

zest of youth. In a gravelly voice he asked me who I had read in the field, and I reeled off the names of some alchemists, such as Albertus Magnus and Paracelsus. He dismissed them with the wave of his pudgy hand.

"'If you wish to accomplish anything, you must upgrade your reading to the latest scholars. Magnus has a wide reach because he's untethered to reality. Read him if you wish to dream.' He scribbled down a list of eight names and handed me the note. 'Read everything you can by these people.'"

Victor's opinion of Krempe increased slightly during the weeks he took his course. Krempe's lack of animation reflected on his students. They dutifully took notes during his lectures, which were not without interest, but uninspiring. Victor vowed to synthesize the ambition of the earlier writers with the specificity of the later ones.

His impression of Professor Waldman was more positive. Waldman was in his 50s, using his smile to encourage students. He came across as a father figure nurturing his son, as opposed to Krempe, who was more like a doubting Thomas. Instead of ridiculing Victor's knowledge of the early natural historians, Waldman praised the young man's diligence, saying any reading was worthwhile if it produced thoughts and ideas. Few of his students had the start that Victor had, and if this was any indication of his drive for the subject, he could go far. Victor usually left Waldman's class feeling good about himself, though that tempered during his studies in his small room. Praise could be helpful, but so was criticism. Victor would take what he could from both.

The portrayal of Waldman in Victor's diaries didn't match the picture Beaulieu gave of a professor who inspired protests. Frankenstein would have to find out for himself.

• • •

Frankenstein walked along the trim campus grounds of the Academy of Geneva. Sunlight scattered through a line of thin poplar trees. Under the more substantial shade of a giant oak, a number of young men sat reading books. Either the men were more open-minded than the average person or the books were engrossing because none of the students paid him any mind. Frankenstein envied their worship of knowledge for knowledge's sake. He had once been such a believer, but now most of his studying went in pursuit of dark truths.

A clerk in the main building told him that Klaus Waldman didn't have a class until late in the afternoon, but he might be found in his cottage on the grounds. As Frankenstein walked up to Waldman's door, he was struck by how pretty and small the cottage was. It seemed confining for a leading professor of natural philosophy, but Waldman probably had access to a laboratory in one of the other university buildings.

The man who answered his knock was short but erect. His ample hair was more salt than pepper. He had a trim beard. At the sight of Frankenstein, his eyes widened, then focused.

"You are Frankenstein's monster," he said in an awed but melodious voice reminiscent of an actor or singer.

"I like to think of myself as *no one's monster but my own*."

Waldman nodded several times. "I heard you were back, and that Victor had died. I am a great admirer of his work."

"His reach extended his grasp."

"That is true of all great researchers. The reach is what leads us to greatness or mediocrity. My work is a shadow compared to his. To finally meet his greatest accomplishment is an honor."

"Not everyone feels that way."

"There will always be doubters. What brings you to my door?" asked Waldman

Frankenstein explained that he was now working as a consulting detective. He told Waldman how Igor had been attacked by someone who was seven feet tall, and that a similarly tall person had been connected with two other attacks. Finally, Frankenstein told him about the possibility that Igor's attacker had been the product of body parts, like himself.

"Is Igor all right?" asked Waldman, concerned.

"Yes. He was able to fight off the assailant. You took an interest in Victor's work. Do you know of anyone else who could create life?"

Waldman smiled wanly. "There was only one Victor. He had a special drive to succeed that took him farther than anyone. Alas, I know of no successors."

Frankenstein frowned. "I have read some of Victor's journals. According to him, you were an influential professor at Ingolstadt. Why have you come to Geneva?"

"Victor may have exaggerated my status. At this point in my career, I've come to appreciate tranquility more than tension that comes from working on the cutting edge of a career field. Geneva, for me, has always represented calm. I'll finish out my career here, then retire, when I hope to appreciate the simple things of nature more than the possibilities of natural philosophy."

Frankenstein, who had spent much of his short existence out of control, felt he understood the man. One thing the detective had learned was, if you didn't control yourself, someone else would, and they wouldn't have your best interests at heart. "I hope you are able to achieve your goals. One last question. Have you had any interaction with Professor Werner Krempe since you left Ingolstadt?"

The affable smile on Waldman's face hardened into a scowl.

"Even during my years at Ingolstadt, I limited my interaction with Krempe. He is someone whose intelligence has been compromised by pessimism."

"Besides yourself, however, he was the professor at Ingolstadt most interested in Victor's work."

"That may be true, but I doubt that interest inspired him to do anything worthwhile. Whatever I've been able to accomplish, my guiding philosophy is *Yes, I can.* Krempe's is, *No, I can't, and neither can you.* I think he was jealous of Victor's accomplishments. With jealousy you waste time lamenting what you don't have instead of taking steps to get what you need."

"So as far as you know, Krempe has not continued Victor's work in recreating human life."

Waldman laughed. "As Krempe is contemptuous of human life, he'd probably decide it wasn't worth the effort. But a few months ago, he left Ingolstadt and, like me, moved to Geneva. You can ask him yourself."

"He's moved to Geneva too? Has he reached out to you?"

Waldman snickered. "The only interaction we've had was three weeks ago. I was walking from my office to my cottage. I heard a cough that reminded me of Krempe's gruff voice. Sure enough, there he was, forty feet away, following me. Our eyes met for a moment, then Krempe turned away, pretending he hadn't seen me. Perhaps he had business at the academy, but knowing Krempe, he might just have wanted to play mind games and follow me around."

Frankenstein reported his findings to Beaulieu and asked if the sheriff had made any progress. Beaulieu said they hadn't been able to find any seven-foot men who were missing a right hand. He added, however, it was interesting that two men connected with Victor Frankenstein had both recently moved to Geneva.

After his meeting with Beaulieu, Frankenstein told Igor he planned to interview Krempe. Learning that Krempe had an arrogant, pessimistic personality, Igor declared he was "My kind of person" and was anxious to meet him.

"What if he was involved in your being assaulted?" asked Frankenstein.

"All the more reason for me to go. It will throw him off guard and show that we can't be intimidated."

"That's not a bad strategy, as long as you don't say something that antagonizes him. We want him to talk to us."

"I will be the picture of decorum," said Igor. "Well, at least in drunken, hunchback circles."

To Frankenstein's knowledge, Igor didn't know any other people with hunchbacks. He did know how to behave himself if the situation demanded it, however, just as he knew how to misbehave when it served his purpose. As for the drinking, Igor would abstain if his wits were required.

•   •   •

Unlike Waldman, Krempe lived in a ramshackle apartment over a pawnshop in one of the seedier areas of Geneva. The uneven, wooden stairs to the second floor creaked under Frankenstein's and Igor's feet. The smell of urine hit their nostrils like a fist.

"I thought professors made money. Isn't that why people study at an academy?" asked Igor.

"Many students already have money before they go to school. As far as we know, Krempe is no longer working as a professor. It does seem odd that he'd choose to uproot himself to live under these circumstances, however."

"Maybe it looks better inside."

When they reached the apartment, Frankenstein rapped on the door. From within they heard a sigh, then the sound of a key turning in the lock. The door opened to the short length of the chain. A short, squat elderly man peered through the crack. His dark hair was straight, worn over his ears, and he had a poorly cut beard that reached his chest.

"Oh my God, it's you!" he said, seeing Frankenstein. "What do you want, you spawn of Satan?"

Frankenstein had been called worse, but he resented being called names by an educated man. "Why did I think academy professors were open-minded?"

"I have no idea," said Krempe. "In most cases, professors merely know more about their narrow-minded pursuits. The information they accumulate serves as a wall rather than a door."

"Are you gentlemen going to have a metaphorical debate on the stairwell or can we come in and discuss my being attacked?" asked Igor.

That was the first moment Krempe had noticed Igor. He muttered, "I see you're spending time in high society. Since I am plainly outnumbered ..."

He unhooked the chain and opened the door, revealing a room strewn with books, notebooks, and loose papers.

"Did we catch you in the middle of something?" asked Frankenstein.

"Yes. My life. Why don't you get to the point and save us all some time?" said Krempe, grabbing an armful of papers and putting them inside a desk drawer against the back wall by a window. The room had a half kitchen to its right with a rickety couch and chair to the left.

Frankenstein considered sitting in the chair, then thought better of it. "Two nights ago, a seven-foot man attacked my friend Igor. He was able to resist, and in the process ripped off the attacker's right hand. Further investigation revealed that this was not the first time the hand had been severed from its body."

"It's just as I thought," said Krempe.

"What is?" asked Frankenstein.

"You think you were a once-in-a-lifetime miracle of natural philosophy? Someone has followed in Victor's footsteps, with the same foul results."

"And maybe that someone is you?" said Igor.

Krempe grimaced. "Me? Why would I do that?"

"You were one of Victor's early admirers," said Frankenstein.

"Yes, but it didn't take me long to realize that his work was unnatural. And if I needed any further confirmation, there was you and the murders you committed."

Frankenstein grabbed Krempe by the soiled collar. "The only person I killed was a young girl, and that was an accident."

"What about poor Henry Clerval? A highly promising student and a model of humanity, cut down in the bloom of youth? What about Elizabeth Lavenza, the one person who could have convinced Victor to use his gifts in a positive way?"

"I did not kill either of those people. Elizabeth saw me in Victor's laboratory and fell down the stairs, hitting her head. I tried to save her. Henry Clerval I've never met."

"Well, I have the word of a monster. That's all there is to it, then. Clerval's death was no accident."

"Neither was me getting attacked by someone who was seven feet tall with detachable hands," said Igor. "Isn't it a coincidence that it happens when a person very interested in Victor's work moves to Geneva?"

Krempe looked at them in contempt. "I don't have to justify myself to anyone, especially you. However, I can't have you interfering with my plans. Have you ever heard of Klaus Waldman?"

"I recently spoke with him," said Frankenstein.

"Then you know why I am here."

"Why don't you enlighten me? Monsters can be slow," said Frankenstein.

"Of course. I will have to go back a bit, and I'll try not to speak too fast. At Ingolstadt I was intrigued by Victor. He was a brilliant man, but he became too full of himself. His plan to create a race of perfect humans made him think he was God. No one has the temperament or wisdom for that. Despite the resulting tragedies, his failure with you was a blessing. Had he succeeded, he would have flooded the earth with supermen and women."

"He hoped to improve upon the people we had," said Frankenstein.

"Of course he did, but they wouldn't have been an improvement. His source material was human, with all its flaws. Victor never had a clear idea of how he was going to make better people, but he was intoxicated by his power to make more of them."

"What's this got to do with you moving to Geneva?" asked Igor.

He glared at the hunchback. "Enlightenment is impossible without patience. Waldman's enthusiasm for Victor's work never waned, and when your creator died, Waldman decided to fill in the gap and moved here. I am determined to stop him."

"Waldman told us he came here for the tranquility. Do you have evidence that he's creating life?" asked Frankenstein.

"I will get it, but I can't confront him directly. If one of his creatures has attacked you, he could have an army behind him by now. But I will expose him, to the point where what passes for law in this city will bring him to justice."

"But why would one of Waldman's creations, if that's what it was, attack Igor?"

"How should I know? Are monsters supposed to be rational? Are people who create them rational?"

"Maybe we can help you," said Frankenstein.

Krempe shook his head. "I work alone."

"Why do you care so much about Waldman now? You didn't do anything to stop Victor," said Igor.

"With knowledge comes responsibility. I know what havoc Waldman could wreak. Though I eventually turned against Victor, I was one of the first professors to encourage him. It's too late for me to be noble. I'm just trying to level my trespasses."

"One last thing," said Frankenstein. "It's none of my business, but you left a job to come here. Geneva's not the cheapest city in the world. How do you make ends meet? It's not from your poems."

Krempe turned away in embarrassment. "No, that's just a hobby. I have ability as a surgeon. Not enough to attach a hand to a body and make it work, but I offer some ... minor procedures. You are right. It's none of your business."

Krempe let the two men out. After the door closed, Igor turned to Frankenstein.

"I wonder if one of the minor procedures Krempe offers is aborting babies," said Igor.

"If so, that would be the opposite of what we suspected him of." Frankenstein took a deep breath and exhaled, his massive chest extending. "I feel like we have three stories here, none of which go together very well. First, you are attacked by someone who is not a normal human being. Second, Waldman moves to Geneva to find calm, blithely denying he has any knowledge about recreating life. The one thing he's not calm about is Krempe, whom he criticizes. Third, Krempe moves here, on a crusade to stop Waldman from creating a super race. Say Krempe is telling the truth. There is nothing in Victor's notes to indicate that Waldman wanted to take over the world. He was always described as a positive, supportive person."

"But that is Victor's point of view," said Igor. "I loved the man, but he was more apt to describe you positively if you agreed with him. It sounds like Waldman did."

"On the other hand, Victor describes Krempe negatively, as a pessimistic, insecure professor who had no qualms about proclaiming your work worthless if it didn't agree with his beliefs. Is he insecure enough to steal Victor's work and blame it on a rival?"

"And why attack me?" asked Igor. "I believe humanity is fatally flawed and can't be improved upon."

Frankenstein smiled. "Yes, you're more negative than either of them. Maybe you staged the attack to shift attention from your attempt to take over the world."

Igor waved his hand dismissively.

"I don't want to take over the world. I just want it to leave me alone."

Their only piece of evidence was a severed hand, thought Frankenstein. If someone had been able to attach the hand in the first place, they might have replaced it by now. Such a person could very well be someone they hadn't met yet. The fact that Victor's two greatest supporters from Ingolstadt had moved to Geneva prior to the attack seemed too great a coincidence to ignore, however. Perhaps he could learn more from Waldman's students.

•   •   •

Frankenstein located the classroom where Waldman taught. From 9:30-10:30 he conducted "Introduction to Chemistry." Frankenstein had hoped to see Waldman in a more demanding course, but being new to the university, he apparently had been stuck with general classes. Careful not to be seen by Waldman, Frankenstein sat outside the room in the hall, listening. Waldman used his sonorous voice to good effect, at least at first. After a while, Frankenstein found his mind wandering and wondered if the same thing was happening with the students. Occasionally, Waldman asked a question, but after pausing a few moments, he inevitably answered it himself.

When the class was dismissed, Frankenstein followed the students outside. A couple of boys gave him strange looks. One of them, a handsome lad with blond hair styled like a bowl pointed at Frankenstein and said to a friend, "I bet you a drink that that man is not a member of the Roundheads."

His friend said, "Quiet, Baptiste. He'll hear you."

"And thanks to you, he'll know my name." Baptiste turned to Frankenstein and said, "I think it's only fair you know that this is Henri Martin." Henri shushed him, then the two burst into laughter. That was good enough for Frankenstein.

"I'm impressed that you know who the Roundheads were. I was wondering if I could ask you boys a few questions."

"Questions?" asked Baptiste. "We've just been subjected to an hour of questions, courtesy of Professor Waldman. I don't think we can take much more."

"Well, this would be an opportunity for you to turn the tables, as my questions concern the professor."

"Who are you?" asked Henri. "We can't just say negative things to anyone who shows up on campus grounds."

"Well, we *could*," said Baptiste, snickering.

"I'm sorry," said Frankenstein. "Of course, you're suspicious, as intelligent young men should be." He reached into his pocket, unfolded a piece of paper, and handed it to Baptiste. "This is signed by Sheriff Beaulieu. Sometimes I assist him."

The two boys looked at the paper.

"Is Professor Waldman in trouble?" asked Baptiste.

"Not at all. I've already talked to him. He is an expert in some areas of chemistry. These areas could help us solve an assault case. We do not believe he is directly involved, as the man described by witnesses doesn't look like him in any way."

"Is there a reward?" asked Henri.

"I don't know anything about that. On the other hand, if you give us helpful information, I'm sure Sheriff Beaulieu would remember it, and it's always an advantage to be on the good side of the law."

Baptiste weighed that and didn't seem too impressed, but then he shrugged. "All right. What do you want to know?"

"I need some background on Professor Waldman, to confirm information he's given us. What is your opinion of him as an educator?"

"Will you tell him what we said?" asked Henri.

"There is no need for that," said Frankenstein. "We just want the truth."

"You can tell him, for all I care," said Baptiste. "He's boring. He talks and talks, and it's as if we're not even there."

"I heard him asking questions," said Frankenstein.

"Yes, but that's after he's put us to sleep. He knows a lot about his subject, but he doesn't know how to teach. He doesn't even act that interested. Every day it seems like his only goal is to get through his boring notes."

"He came from Ingolstadt highly regarded," said Frankenstein.

"Really? I thought that was supposed to be a good school, but maybe they have lower standards than we have," said Henri.

"Another thing. He's frightened of students," said Baptiste. "He doesn't look them in the eye. He has a decent speaking voice, but he gets nervous. He forgets that he says something and says it again. About three weeks ago he gave us the same lecture he'd given the class the day before. No one bothered to tell him."

"Less work for us," said Henri.

"Right, but we are paying for his services. We're not getting our money's worth."

"Do the rest of the students feel that way?" asked Frankenstein.

"Definitely," said Henri. "You can tell if someone likes teaching or not. Waldman would rather be somewhere else."

And yet, he traveled many miles to teach at the Academy of Geneva. None of this matched Victor's impressions of

Waldman. Were the students in Geneva different, or had Waldman changed? Frankenstein shook hands with the two boys. "Thank you. You've been very helpful. Rest assured I will not share your names with Professor Waldman."

Baptiste smiled. "And if you do, we can always share your name with the authorities for scaring people at the academy. Frankenstein."

The boy had read Beaulieu's note. He might have a good future.

•   •   •

"Something's bothering Waldman," Frankenstein said to Igor as the two sat in Igor's small room. "He told us he came to Geneva for tranquility, but he doesn't seem to have found it."

"I don't know anything about being a professor," said Igor. "But I would think with someone who has taught for as long as he has, it would get easier. Maybe as he gets older he has less in common with his students."

"No doubt, but everybody gets older, if they're lucky. Not every good professor suddenly gets bad. Another interesting thing about both Waldman and Krempe is neither of them have families."

"Neither do we."

"Right, but Waldman and Krempe don't look like us," said Frankenstein.

"I could have a family if I wanted to. I don't want to take on the responsibility."

"I'm sure your prospective spouse wouldn't, either. I'll check if either of them ever got married. If so, we can track down the ex-spouses and maybe get a written statement from them. If Waldman is behind these attacks, whatever he's nervous about could be the reason why."

"So you don't think it's Krempe?" asked Igor.

"He's not likeable, but he never was. At least he's matching the portrait Victor painted of him, unlike Waldman. Of course, he could just be trying to shift the blame on his former colleague."

•   •   •

A misty rain fell as Krempe stood outside the building that housed Victor Frankenstein's laboratory. Though it was mid-afternoon, the fog made it seem dark as dusk. The three-story structure stood bent but not bowed, a portion of back roof caved in slightly. The tiny windows dotting the house were opaque with dirt. The wooden steps to the front door set deep and uneven in the wet ground.

Before Victor created the monster, Krempe never would have suspected Waldman of creating life from body parts. When the monster had first been unleashed and committed its murders, Waldman had pretended to be shocked. He'd told Krempe that he wrote a lengthy letter to Victor imploring him to give up his experiments before it was too late. Krempe had only Waldman's word for that, however. He could have written a very different letter, asking to become Victor's assistant. Why else did Waldman move to Geneva if not to follow in Victor's misguided footsteps?

Not for a moment did Krempe believe Waldman came because he wanted to find peace. In the very city where the monster was unleashed? It made no sense. It was too dangerous for Waldman to conduct the experiments at the academy, however, and his apartment was too small. Everyone thought the Frankenstein house was abandoned. It was the perfect place for Waldman to work unimpeded.

Krempe grasped the rusted metal handle of the door and pulled down. The door was unlocked, though he had to push hard to open it. The dark inside forced him to light his lantern. Elaborate spider webs connected the ceiling and cupboards of a dusty kitchen. No one had cooked anything here in a long time. The kitchen connected to a living room, equally decorated by spiders. He gasped as his face hit one of the unyielding webs.

Dust covered a three-cushioned couch and three plush chairs. Bookcases flush with old volumes lined the walls. He noticed many notebooks, and not many empty spaces. Surely, Waldman would have taken some of these?

Worried that perhaps his suspicions of Waldman were unfounded, Krempe thought perhaps the proof would be in the basement. The door downstairs creaked as he opened it. With one hand holding out the lantern, the other grasping the unstable railing, he cautiously descended.

It was all there. The lab, the platform on which the body of the monster had laid, the conductors to attract the lightning, the wires and machines to animate the body. A lumpy, dirty sheet covered the platform, but it was otherwise empty. He needed evidence that work was being done. Where would it be hidden? For that matter, why would it be hidden? From the looks of this place, no one had been in here in years.

"Who are you?" a deep, barely feminine voice asked.

He nearly jumped out of his skin. Whirling around, he faced a seven-foot tall woman with dark hair piled up like a beehive. She wore a white, sheet-like robe that made her look like a ghost.

"I could ask you the same question. This is the property of Victor Frankenstein," said Krempe.

"And you are not he."

"True, but if you are what I think you are, you have no right to be anywhere except in the ground. Did Professor Waldman create you?"

The woman smiled coldly. "You read too many fantastic novels."

Krempe didn't read any fantastic novels, but if he had, he was sure they wouldn't help him now. How could he have been so overconfident? All those years he'd spent isolated as a professor, as a researcher. How many times had he discounted contrary views simply because they were contrary? He still had a brilliant mind. He needed to use it to get out of here.

"I was one of the first people to see the potential of Victor Frankenstein."

The woman laughed loudly. "You are seeing it now."

She wasn't even bothering to deny it. She had no intention of letting him leave. If she was anything like the first Frankenstein monster, she would possess superhuman strength. It was all down to timing now. When she was off guard, he would run for it. But those eyes, bereft of sympathy, bore down on him without interruption.

He had no weapon. He backed a little closer to a bookcase. Books had always been the answer for him. A heavy tome heaved into her face would buy him a few seconds. It could make a difference. He whirled around and extricated a tall, thick black volume and threw it at her. He heard her grunt as he dashed for the stairs. He had gone only a few steps when the arms of another giant clamped on him. His brain summoned up a childhood memory: The family cat with a tiny bird riding between its jaws, the captive looking relaxed and resigned.

•   •   •

For Igor, the next morning didn't start until the afternoon. His appearance had made him a night person by habit. His other habit, drinking, when Frankenstein wasn't depending on him for anything, also contributed to his late rising.

He swung his legs onto the floor, then came the hard part, raising his head. The pain was unpleasant but not debilitating. As he stood up, his eyes fell on an envelope pushed under his door. Frankenstein must have something for him to do. He picked it up. Usually Frankenstein wrote "Igor" on his envelopes, but this one was bare. Tearing it open, he saw this message on a neatly folded piece of paper.

"I apologize for my rude behavior during our meeting. I have learned many things, but social niceties are not one of them. One of my goals in coming to Geneva is to make the world a better place. As I said, in my years I have accumulated some surgical skill. While I could not make your hunchback completely disappear, I could diminish it, with little danger to yourself. If you are interested, please meet me for a consultation at my apartment tonight at 9 p.m."

It was signed, *Krempe.*

•   •   •

Igor brought Krempe's note to Frankenstein's office.

"He wants to make the world a better place? That's hilarious," said Igor. "And why would Krempe reach out to me? When you offered to help with his investigation of Waldman, he practically threw us out."

"He'd have to know that you'd show me the note," said Frankenstein. "If he didn't want you to do that, he could have said to come to his apartment this morning."

"So what do we do? I'm not really in the mood for invasive surgery."

"He said consultation. Let's see what he wants."

At 9 p.m. they were back at Krempe's doorstep. Frankenstein knocked, but there was no answer. He tried the door and found it unlocked. The two entered the apartment. It was dark inside, and the books and papers on the floor made walking treacherous.

"You'd think people would put lanterns where you could find them," said Igor.

"The advantage of being an inhabitant is you know where to look," said Frankenstein.

"Right, but you have to be home to take advantage of that advantage."

"I have a bad feeling about this."

"I have several."

None of this made any sense, thought Frankenstein. In their only meeting Krempe had been contemptuous of Igor. Also, what doctor held consultations this late in the day? Only those who were up to no good.

"Krempe, are you here?" asked Frankenstein.

"God's heart!" said Igor, tripping over something.

"What happened?"

Igor reached down and felt a wet, bloody body.

●　　　●　　　●

Beaulieu liked to go to bed early when his job allowed. He thought it was unnatural to stay up long after dark. He was not happy to be woken, and less happy to have to spend time with a corpse. He, Frankenstein, and Igor had each brought a lantern, filling up Krempe's already cluttered apartment with shadows. The professor's body, a knife sticking out of his belly, lay in a pool of blood.

"So, Krempe invited Igor to his home for a nocturnal operation," said Beaulieu.

"He apparently started without us," said Igor.

"And you think Waldman, or some super creature he's created, might have done this?" asked Beaulieu.

"Supposedly, Krempe has been harrying Waldman," said Frankenstein. "He hasn't been in Geneva that long. If he has other enemies, he made them quickly."

"Apparently, he had some skill in that regard," said Igor.

"Whoever killed him wanted us to know about it," said Frankenstein.

Beaulieu had never had much use for academy-educated people. In his opinion, they spent years learning more and more about things that had little impact on real life. The one good thing about people with degrees is they tended to commit fewer crimes than uneducated people. It appeared this could be the exception that proved the rule. "All right. I will have someone collect Professor Krempe," said Beaulieu. "In the meantime, let's pay a visit to Professor Waldman."

•　　•　　•

"I've been home since 5 p.m.," said a disheveled Waldman when he opened his door to Beaulieu, Frankenstein, and Igor.

"Can anyone confirm that?" asked Beaulieu.

"I live alone. I'm middle-aged. I didn't hire a prostitute for the night."

"You don't have any supermen hanging around that can speak for you?" asked Beaulieu.

"What are you talking about?" asked Waldman.

"It's what my two friends are talking about," said Beaulieu. "They think that you may have gotten into the people-creating business, following in the footsteps of Victor Frankenstein. You deny that?"

Waldman laughed. "Of course I do. As I told them, I came to Geneva for calm. There was nothing calm about Victor's life in his last years."

"Could you tell me about your recent interaction with Werner Krempe?" asked Beaulieu.

"Ah, I suspect he is the reason for these wild accusations. He was following me here on campus. If it happened again, I would have taken out a complaint against him."

"It's a little late for that," said Beaulieu. "We found him in his apartment this evening, dead."

Waldman froze. "When did it happen? I had nothing to do with it. I told you I have been here since 5 p.m."

Beaulieu glanced at Frankenstein and Igor. "Well, I'm the kind of person that wants to trust people. It would make my job so much easier if everyone just told each other the truth. But being an officer of the law, people lie to me every day. So, could we come in and look around?"

"I'd rather you didn't. The house is a mess," said Waldman.

"That's all right. We prefer messy houses. They generate more clues," said Beaulieu, pushing past Waldman. Frankenstein and Igor followed.

The three men searched the kitchen and living room. Despite Waldman's protest that the house was a mess, Beaulieu was surprised how clean and orderly the place was, considering Waldman lived alone. The books that jammed his three bookcases had sections, arranged by author's last name. A closed notebook had been left on top of a desk. A glass contained a number of writing utensils. Beaulieu was about to open the bedroom door when Waldman put his hand on the sheriff's shoulder.

"I'd prefer you not go in there," said Waldman.

"I see that," said Beaulieu. "Can you present a convincing argument as to why I shouldn't?"

Waldman hesitated, turned away as if he were trying to

think of something to say, then faced Beaulieu. "I didn't exactly tell you the truth earlier."

"My theory about humanity borne out once again," said Beaulieu.

"I—there is a woman with whom I spend time with," Waldman stammered. "It would be a hardship for her if her identity was revealed. Not everyone is open-minded about this sort of thing."

"Is it a student?" asked Igor.

"Of course not. Look, you want to get to the bottom of Krempe's death. Involving this woman will only complicate matters."

"Sorry, professor," said Beaulieu. "At this point, we need more evidence, not less." He opened the bedroom door. Frankenstein lit the gas light inside. A rumpled double bed dominated the room. They checked under the bed and in two closets. Inside one of them Igor pulled out a blouse stained with blood. There was no woman.

"Is this yours?" Beaulieu asked, holding it up.

Waldman looked away. "No."

"Professor, I think it would be better if we continued our discussion at the police station," said Beaulieu.

•　　　•　　　•

Frankenstein and Beaulieu entered the interrogation room, where Waldman sat at a table, exhausted. A half empty glass of water and an inkwell were set on a wooden table.

"Where's the gentleman with the hunchback? He doesn't have any questions to ask me?" asked Waldman.

"We didn't want to gang up on you too much," said Beaulieu. He and Frankenstein sat in two of the empty chairs. Beaulieu placed a notebook on the table, opened it to a blank page, and pulled out a pen. "Talk."

Waldman scratched his beard and sat forward in his chair. Its legs scraped the floor. "The blouse belongs to Catarina. At least, that's what she calls herself these days."

"It's not her original name?" asked Beaulieu.

"Originally, she didn't have a name."

"She is someone you created," said Frankenstein.

"Yes and no."

"This is not the time for doubletalk, Waldman," said Beaulieu.

"Agreed," said Waldman. "This woman was created by Victor Frankenstein."

"I don't think so," said Frankenstein. "The only other person he created was a mate that I asked for. His hatred for me made him destroy her."

"And my envy of him made me resuscitate her," Waldman said flatly.

"That's impossible," said Frankenstein, though he knew it wasn't. Conflicting emotions filled his head.

"Don't underestimate the power of envy," said Waldman. "Every time I encouraged Victor, a part of me wanted him to fail. When he succeeded with you, I knew what I wanted to do. When I learned that he died, there was nothing to stop me from reading Victor's notebooks and following in his footsteps. Nothing except ... common sense, decency!"

"How long has she been resuscitated?" asked Frankenstein.

"Six months," said Waldman. "The worst six months of my life."

"So where is she?" asked Beaulieu.

Waldman shrugged. "It doesn't matter. She will be back."

"Did you sew a hand on her?" asked Frankenstein.

"She's not the type of thing you can say *no* to."

"So, you did whatever she asked," said Beaulieu.

Waldman's eyes dropped. "Yes."

"What else did she ask?" said Frankenstein.

"At first, I was just her doctor. I didn't realize she was killing people. When I found out and refused to keep helping her, she threatened to tell you everything, that it was my fault she killed because I'd repaired her. She also threatened to ruin my reputation. But I don't care anymore!"

"Ruin it how?" asked Frankenstein.

"She has ... needs. I was forced to satisfy them as best I could."

"Oh God," said Beaulieu.

"Did she attack Igor?" Frankenstein asked.

"Yes."

"Why?" asked Frankenstein.

Waldman smiled bitterly. "Because he is your friend and she wants revenge on you."

"Why would she want revenge on me? If I hadn't asked Victor to make me a mate, she wouldn't exist."

"That's one of the things she holds against you," said Waldman. "The other is the fact that you killed Victor."

"I never laid a hand on him! He died chasing me across the Arctic!"

Waldman shrugged. "I never said she was rational." He turned to Beaulieu. "Look, do whatever you want with me. I don't care, as long as you don't let me loose. I'll have more freedom in a cell than I have on the outside."

Frankenstein and Beaulieu left the interrogation room.

"I can hold him for lying to the police, but it appears he's not the main problem," said Beaulieu.

"No," said Frankenstein. "And I'm the one who needs to deal with it. I know a thing or two about anger and the type of isolation Catarina is probably feeling. I was able to deal with it. Maybe I can help her do the same."

"It's a little late for that, isn't it? She's killed a man, and others, according to Waldman. I don't give a damn about her emotional wellbeing."

"Maybe not, but I might be able to use it to everyone's advantage," said Frankenstein. "I suggest you release Waldman. He definitely doesn't want to go anywhere near Catarina, but she might expose herself going back to him, especially if she knows he's talked to us."

"Sounds reasonable. I'll have one of my men keep a close watch on him."

Frankenstein returned to his home. He dropped onto his bed, the springs protesting. His last thought was, I'm tired.

• • •

He didn't wake up until 10:30 a.m. With his job he was used to keeping all sorts of hours, but mid-morning still seemed an odd time to start a day. He'd dreamed that he was arguing with Victor about whether or not to destroy Catarina. He, the monster, maintained that it was unnatural to be the only one of its kind. Victor wouldn't budge. The bride had to be destroyed.

It reminded the detective of one of Victor's most significant flaws: he was a terrible listener. Plus, he was consumed more by humanity's opinion of him than by a desire to improve it. "You can't undo what you have done!" Frankenstein shouted at his creator, just before he woke up.

He made himself a breakfast of bread, butter, milk, and strawberries and sat down at his dining room table. While eating he heard the hinge on his mail slot go up and click down. That was odd, as normally, his mail didn't arrive until 2 p.m. He picked up a single envelope on the floor. It had no address on it. He ripped it open. A single piece of paper had the following message:

"If you wish to see Igor again, come ALONE to the Frankenstein laboratory at 8 p.m."

Frankenstein unlocked the door and ran onto the street. To his right, about a hundred feet away, he saw a tiny man in a flat cap.

"Hey!" Frankenstein yelled.

The man broke into a run. His stride was about half that of Frankenstein's, and the detective soon grabbed him by the shoulder. The man was middle-aged, balding, and filthy. His unshaven face was gray and bristly.

"I just delivered the letter! I don't know anything about it!" he gasped.

"Who gave it to you?" asked Frankenstein.

"A tall woman. Not my type. She paid me. I didn't care who she was or what the letter said."

Frankenstein released the man. He was right. He knew nothing.

• • •

As Frankenstein rode in a horse cart to the place of his creation, he thought about Igor. They had a lot in common. To most people Igor was defined by his hunchback, just as many people saw Frankenstein's huge body and thought: "Monster." Few people other than Victor and Frankenstein would hire Igor, which made him dependent. Frankenstein had spent the first years of his life burning in flames of hatred. Both of them had eventually chosen a more positive path than could have been predicted. He couldn't have found a more loyal, hardworking assistant than Igor.

But now Igor was in trouble, and it was because of his relationship with Frankenstein. Frankenstein could not be responsible for another death. He had told Beaulieu to post himself outside Victor's laboratory at 9 p.m. That would give Frankenstein an hour to try and solve this problem, without Catarina seeing that he'd enlisted help. Frankenstein told Beaulieu to use his own judgment about when to enter.

It had been years since Frankenstein had fled the laboratory. Seeing it now, he assumed, was like seeing a primary school through the eyes of an adult. He saw ghosts of himself, strapped to a bench, walking through the building's rooms and learning, asking an impatient Victor countless questions.

He was all feelings at that point, untethered by experience or reading. Today his emotions were more subdued, for which he was thankful. A jagged bolt of lightning illuminated the night, flashing the three-story house in his eyes, replacing his memory. A distant rumble of thunder sounded softly, and he felt his neck tingle.

He knocked on the front door.

After a minute or two, it slowly opened, revealing Catarina. As he stood at the bottom of the steps, she towered over him. Her black hair was piled on top of her head. Her eyes were piercing. She wore a loose, white robe.

"We meet again," she said.

"Where is Igor?"

"Where he belongs, in the lab, the one place he can call home."

"Have you harmed him?" asked Frankenstein.

"I needed to apply some force to convince him to come with me, but I doubt anyone will pay much attention to the bruise on the side of his head."

"What do you want from me?" The air had become misty.

"Come in and I will explain," she said softly.

She led him into the living room, though it showed no signs of recent life. Dust covered the furniture. Cracks disfigured the wall. She motioned for him to sit on the lumpy couch. She sat in a chair, its cushion ripped.

"I just can't stay away from this place," she said.

"It has no pull over me," said Frankenstein.

"That's because you deny who you are. I can understand why. I'd had such a short life. Barely time to form any opinions. My eyes opened inside this laboratory. I was strapped to that table, and all I saw were clanking machines, endless wires, and sizzling electricity. A Romanticist's nightmare, and yet, the only thing I felt was a sense of wonder at this thing called life. And the first two people I saw were you and Victor. Victor's eyes were aghast, and I didn't know why. Yours, on the other hand, looked at me with hope, care, maybe even love. Why didn't you protect me?"

"I didn't know he was going to destroy you. He'd gone to all the trouble to create you."

"You knew how he felt about *you*! You forced him to make me! How could you *not* know?"

"Victor created life not because he wanted to make it better. He wanted to be God. And so he was, for you and me. But someone with the power of God needs to be perfect. He could never be that. At the time I didn't think his hubris would allow him to destroy his creation."

"Really. You never read about Noah's ark?" asked Catarina.

"Like I said, *at the time*."

"You are right about one thing. Victor is God to me, and that God ranted and raved about what an abomination I was. I hadn't had time to be anything, but he said I had ruined his life. It was bad enough that he created one monster. He wasn't going to allow another to damn his existence. He came at me with a knife. I was still restrained to that table. I felt him plunge the blade in my heart."

"I'm sorry."

Catarina laughed. "Do you honestly think your feelings have any effect on me now? I, the product of one man's regrets? You are the reason I exist!"

"I know that."

"This hatred I feel is because of you."

"I had to fight that hatred as well. You can let it envelop you, or you can try to control it."

"How would you suggest I do that?"

"Read books. Help people."

"Did reading books help you?" she asked.

"Not at first. It just increased my awareness of how unfair life was. And my response was similar to yours: anger. And the focus of that anger was Victor. I delighted in uprooting his life. I taunted him. I led him on a chase of hate across the world. I thought I was in control, but I wasn't. I was running as fast as he was. I just happened to be in front of him. When he died, it was because of his hatred of me and himself. It gave me no satisfaction. The same thing will happen if you kill me. Your anger will continue unabated."

"Every person who looks down on me is my enemy. I won't run out of targets." She sneered.

"You can have my life, if you can take it. But release Igor. He is blameless."

"He is not! He was Victor's assistant, and now he is yours. I'm not here to make a deal."

He could see that. Beaulieu was not scheduled to show up for another three quarters of an hour. Frankenstein had some time to kill before Catarina tried to kill him.

"Let me see Igor. How do I know he's even here?" asked Frankenstein.

"Oh, you'll know," she said. "You're going to take his place. Let's take a walk back down to the womb for such as us. I assume you remember the way."

She motioned for Frankenstein to walk in front of her. Though one had to descend stairs to get to the laboratory, its ceiling went up to the roof. Catarina's lantern barely carved out a cave of light in the darkness. She lit three lanterns in the laboratory, the flickering light giving the machinery a threatening appearance. Fidgeting in its corners, wheezing, muttering, scratching, were ten people, five men and five women. They had the decayed look of zombies, except they showed no interest in Frankenstein's flesh. Frankenstein saw the battered body of Igor stretched supine against a reclined padded bench. His arms and legs were restrained with chains.

"Are you all right?" asked Frankenstein, walking up to the bench.

"I've had better accommodations," he muttered, his voice weak. "This is definite proof that Victor didn't hit the bull's eye every time. This woman has a death wish. I say we grant it."

Catarina slapped Igor's face, causing him to yelp. "Don't talk as if I wasn't here."

"Wishful thinking," he gasped.

"Who are these other people?" asked Frankenstein.

"My assistants," said Catarina.

"They don't look very energetic."

"They can be if I demand it. The best part of their existence is to come. Up to now, they have never left the building. Once they leave, they won't be satisfied staying inside."

"Did Waldman create them?" asked Frankenstein. "It's hard to believe."

"Professor Waldman may be a weak man, but he has an above average intellect. He has been able to follow in Victor's footsteps, if not lead. Come here, Waldman."

Frankenstein saw a man walk out of the shadows.

"I'm afraid I had to kill the man who was watching him," said Catarina.

Frankenstein wondered if Beaulieu would be on time. If one of his men had been killed, he was probably dealing with that.

"Don't you have a mind of your own, Waldman?" asked Igor. "What's the point of all your education if you're going to use it for someone like her?"

Catarina slapped Igor in the face again, a little harder this time. "I assure you my arm has enough strength to answer every insult you hurl at me. You won't dislodge my hand a second time."

A burst of lightning lit up the windows, followed by a loud crack of thunder.

"That storm isn't far away," said Frankenstein.

"Very observant," said Catarina. "Here is my offer. I will let Igor live if you take his place on the bench. You'll notice that the wires are set up to lead the electricity from the storm to the top of the bench. That's where your head will be."

"I don't see the point in that. The electricity initially gave us life, but as far as I know, getting electrocuted will just kill me."

"Correct, but I neglected to tell you one important detail. You will already be dead. Professor Waldman is going to substitute your brain for another, more deserving one."

Frankenstein didn't doubt her seriousness, though he couldn't imagine which brain could be more deserving, unless it was the one that was originally in his body. That would be far too humanitarian of Catarina. He did know there was no way he would allow his body to be reanimated with another brain. He assumed he would be unaware of it, but the notion of him walking around, doing things he would have no control over? He had spent enough of his short life being out of control.

"Whose brain are you talking about?" he asked. "And why do you need to put it in my body? Why don't you put it in your body? You don't seem to like life very much."

Catarina shook her head. "I want this person to understand me, and being in my body without my point of view wouldn't convey what I must convey. You see, the brain belonged to Victor Frankenstein."

"That's impossible. Victor died in the Arctic. His body is in the bottom of the ocean."

"His body? Yes! But you know what an egotist Victor was. He convinced the ship's doctor to preserve his brain."

"And you were able to convince the doctor to give it to you?"

"I can be very persuasive, but it didn't come to that. An enterprising sailor stole it from the doctor, who sold it to me."

"But Victor died years ago! How could anyone preserve a brain that long?"

"In a preservative solution, isn't it possible?" asked Catarina.

It could be, for all Frankenstein knew. "Even if it is, how do you know it's Victor's brain?"

Catarina glared. "He had Victor's ring. He knew details about the ship Victor died on."

Frankenstein laughed. "You've been tricked. Even if it is Victor's brain, there's no guarantee he'll remember anything. I have no memories prior to when I was reanimated."

"Waldman has reanimated other people for me. They have retained their memories."

"Did you put other people's preserved brains into them?"

"No, it wasn't necessary. We got their bodies quickly." She put her face inches from his. "Doubts are for weaklings. You're not going to put them into my mind. If you want to save Igor's life, you will have to sacrifice your own."

"Let him go first," said Frankenstein.

"After you've been restrained and ... sedated."

There was no reason to trust Catarina. Igor was uncharacteristically quiet, just watching everything, but if he was released, he wouldn't rest until Catarina was punished.

"I gave you a choice," said Catarina. "If you don't want it, that's fine with me." She turned to the ten reanimates. "Move Igor to the chain by the wall. Put Frankenstein in his place."

Waldman and two reanimates approached Igor. Waldman unlocked the bonds while the two minions wrestled Igor to a chain stapled to the wall. Though the reanimates weren't tall like Frankenstein, they were strong. The remaining eight grabbed Frankenstein. He kicked one in the face. It grabbed his upraised leg, while two others clamped onto his arms. He was wrestled to the floor and dragged to the bench, secured by a chain. Frankenstein tried to resist, but even he couldn't stop the combined strength of the reanimates.

As he lay supine, Catarina stood over him. "You've lived your life alone. There is strength in numbers."

A burst of lightning lit up the laboratory, followed by a blast of rolling thunder.

Frankenstein said, "If you wanted to follow Victor's example, why didn't you make the reanimates superhuman size?"

"Waldman and I decided that was an ego-driven mistake. If you want to get something done, you don't cultivate an appearance that draws attention to itself." She turned to Waldman. "You'd better get started."

Waldman pushed a cart laden with knives and scalpels. Some were flecked with blood.

"Those don't look very clean," said Frankenstein.

"I wouldn't worry about it," said Waldman, picking up a syringe. "If there are any repercussions, you won't be aware of them."

Frankenstein's life had been difficult. From the onset, he'd met with disapproval and horror. Many times in combating these things, he'd felt a lack of purpose. But at the moment he felt a new feeling: helplessness. His life was going to be ended by a weakling. Or, perhaps it was inaccurate to give Waldman that much credit. He was a coerced follower. All Frankenstein could do was keep asking questions. If talking to Victor was so important to Catarina, he had to make her keep talking.

"Why resurrect Victor when he never wanted to create you in the first place?" Frankenstein asked.

Catarina scowled. "But he did, and he must take responsibility for that. I am under no illusion that I will get his love, but I will get his apology. God will apologize to me."

"Then what?"

"Then I will take his place."

Frankenstein grimaced as he felt Waldman's syringe prick his arm. Waldman whispered into Frankenstein's ear. "Pretend that you are unconscious." Surreptitiously, the professor placed a key into Frankenstein's right hand.

Was this a trick? If these were the last seconds of his life, Frankenstein wanted to spend them with his eyes open. He knew certain drugs could knock one out within seconds. He waited, then glanced up at Waldman, trying to catch his eye. Waldman didn't look at him, instead adjusting the wires that were connected to the bench and the lightning rods on the roof of the laboratory.

There was another burst of lightning, so close Frankenstein thought he could hear the electricity, followed by an angry rumble of thunder.

"Hurry up, Waldman," said Catarina. "Can you even see what you're doing? The storm is already getting close. It will have passed by the time you place Victor's brain into the monster."

"Be patient. A series of thunderstorms will pass through tonight. If we miss this one, there will be another," said Waldman. "I just need to adjust the wires. They aren't properly grounded." Catarina watched impatiently as Waldman held up the wires and hesitated.

"What are you doing? This isn't the time ..."

She was interrupted by another lightning burst. The energy crackled down the wires, racing like a controlled avalanche. Waldman screamed as he lunged toward Catarina, wrapping his arms around her. The two of them spun like a top, then fell to the ground. The floor burst into fire.

Not again, thought Frankenstein. The reanimates chattered like monkeys without any sense of direction. Frankenstein inserted the key into the chain lock, urging his clumsy fingers to obey him. The lock clicked open. He threw the chain to the ground and rushed to Igor. The key fell to the ground, but he scooped it up and freed his friend, dragging him to the far end of the laboratory. They'd never make it to the main entrance, but there was a bulkhead in the back from which they might escape.

Frankenstein's actions were decisive, but the truth was, fire terrified him. It spread greedily, consuming everything in its path. He pushed the confused reanimates out of his way. Climbing up the back stairs, he fought with the hot and unyielding bolt that locked the bulkhead. With a gasp, he threw it open, pushed up the doors, and burst into the night air.

From a safe distance he and Igor stared at the burning laboratory, the screams of the reanimates ringing over the crackling flames. Rain pelted down, but it had little effect on the interior of the building. Frankenstein looked helplessly at Igor.

"Let them die," said Igor. "They did once already."

"I can't," said Frankenstein.

He rushed back to the bulkhead, its right door hanging open on one hinge. The smoke and flames made his view of the interior fragmented, like a fevered dream. One of the steps collapsed as he gingerly stepped back into the building, dropping him to his hands and knees. The screams rang out unabated, but he couldn't see anyone, making him unsure if he was the source. A flaming wooden beam crashed to the floor, missing him by inches. He didn't want to die, but perhaps this was an appropriate ending. He would go down with the destruction of the laboratory that begot him.

Then he saw one of them, just standing there, ten feet away. Shorter than the others, her long brown hair askew, her eyes resigned. He would remember the totality of that resignation. He scooped her up and staggered out of the building.

·　　·　　·

The next thing Frankenstein knew, Beaulieu was standing over them. The rain had stopped as suddenly as it began.

"Are you all right?" Beaulieu asked.

Frankenstein looked down at his soot-blackened clothes. "We're a bit crispy, but we're still breathing."

"The fire's too far gone for us to do anything about it. Is there anyone still inside?" Beaulieu asked.

"Waldman, ten reanimated people. I managed to get one out." He pointed to the unconscious soot-covered woman.

"What was Waldman trying to do?" asked Beaulieu.

"It wasn't Waldman's plan. He was used by Catarina, a reanimated monster, like me. She was going to kill me, then insert Victor's brain into my head."

Beaulieu shook his head. "Why can't you people leave things alone?"

•   •   •

The fire burned until the late morning. The reanimates had returned to the death they'd been snatched from, or at least most of them had. Beaulieu's men found the remains of only eight bodies. One of them could have been Waldman, as the bodies were burnt beyond recognition, though none were tall enough to be Catarina. That left two unaccounted for.

Frankenstein had thought both Waldman and Catarina had been killed by the lightning bolt. But what if one of the reanimates had escaped with the body of Catarina? Could she be resuscitated a second time? Who could do it, with Waldman dead? Who *would* do it? Would the reanimate have the presence of mind to also rescue Victor's brain? These were all questions a part of him hoped would never be answered. He resisted Beaulieu's suggestion he see a doctor and instead went home, cleaned up, and slept.

That evening Frankenstein, at his insistence, helped Beaulieu interrogate the surviving reanimate. With her rotted flesh, she was a fright to begin with. They'd cleaned her up, but they couldn't do much about her hair, most of which had been burnt away by the fire. Frankenstein felt sorry for her as she fidgeted in her chair at the table.

"Do you have a name?" asked Beaulieu.

The reanimate's mouth creased. "It used to be Abby."

"How did you die?"

"I was a prostitute. The last thing I remember before I was reanimated was getting stabbed by a man who didn't want to pay me."

"How long ago did this happen?" asked Beaulieu.

"I don't know. What is today's date?" Beaulieu told her. "Then it was four months ago."

"And what have you been doing since then?"

She shrugged. "The bidding of Catarina. I assisted in the creation of other reanimates as far as fetching utensils. I made dinner, swept. Much of the time I did nothing."

"How do you feel about being alive?" asked Frankenstein.

"I don't know anything about being dead, though apparently, I was. Catarina made sure we all understood that we were alive thanks to her. That was enough for us to follow her orders, except for one man. He resisted, saying he had not asked her to intervene in his death, and so he owed her nothing. We killed him."

"You personally?" asked Beaulieu.

"I helped hold him down."

"Catarina told me she intended to put the brain of my creator into my body so she could get an apology," said Frankenstein. "Did she share with you any other future plans?"

"She hated everything. She wanted revenge against the human race, but she was never clear on how she was going to get it, or what good it was going to do her."

"Do you feel hate?" asked Frankenstein. "

Abby searched for words. "No. Just emptiness."

People like Victor and Catarina had harnessed the power of life, Frankenstein thought, yet they gave no thought to their creations' quality of life. At least an author's characters had no life beyond a book. These poor souls had to defend themselves against a world seemingly without morals or care.

After the interrogation, Beaulieu had Abby taken back to her cell.

"How much of all this is going to be told?" asked Frankenstein. "About Waldman, Catarina, the reanimates?"

Beaulieu folded his large arms. "My job is to see that justice prevails. Catarina killed some people, but you think she's dead. The other reanimates shouldn't have been brought back alive, and now they're dead. At least nine of them. Waldman aided and abetted Catarina, and he's dead. That's more closure than we normally get."

"In the end Waldman was also a hero. His family deserves to know that, and despite his mistakes, he deserves that as well. If not for him, I'd be dead, or worse. Plus, if this doesn't come out, then someone else might get the horrible idea of bringing the dead back to life. Transparency has worked for me."

"You do what you have to do."

"And what about Abby?"

"I can't hold her much longer, but I don't know what else to do with her," said Beaulieu.

"Looking like that, she can't go back to being a prostitute," said Frankenstein.

"Unfortunately, I don't know if that's so. Most people don't hire prostitutes based on their looks. I wish she could have told us more about Catarina."

"We may learn more yet. Abby is, at least in part, an example of her handiwork. That tells us a lot about who she was."

"I'm not going to charge her for killing someone who was already dead, but what's going to happen to her when I cut her loose?" asked Beaulieu.

Frankenstein frowned.

"I'll take her on for a while. It's the least I can do."

• • •

It was a bit crowded at Frankenstein's flat, but he had to admit, he didn't mind the company. He bought her a brown wig. That and makeup improved her appearance. She found each morning a trial.

"I don't know how to start," she said at the breakfast table. "I don't know who I am."

"That's always a work in progress," said Frankenstein.

There would be difficulties ahead. No one knew that better than he. People would hate her. Many would accuse her of being an abomination. He had not been able to save Catarina, but for as long as Abby would let him, he would help her fight her fights. In one way he had been blessed. There was no shortage of good things that needed to be done.

ABOUT THE AUTHOR

Richard Zwicker is a retired English teacher living in Vermont, USA, with his wife and beagle. His short stories have appeared in *Heroic Fantasy Quarterly*, *Stupefying Stories*, *Dragon Gems*, and other semi-pro markets. Two collections of his work, *Walden Planet and other stories* and *The Reopened Cask and other stories* are also available. In addition to reading and writing, he likes to play the piano, jog, and fight the good fight against what he used to call middle age.